Call of an Angry Blackbird

JONATHAN LOVEJOY

Armageddon Publishing
All rights reserved.

Cover: *Italian Girl at the Fountain*, 1870
William Adolphe Bouguereau (1825-1905)

ISBN-10: 069235932X
ISBN-13: 978-0692359327

For every Elizabeth

Rising above the trees of life

Despairs lift Autumn's fervent night

Burdens of pain in weary strife—

Drift beneath the Harvest Moon

PART ONE

1

Far away, over distant places, the Winds continue their journey. They travel across the oceans and mountain ranges. Blowing down into the valleys and above the open plains. Forever Seeking. Searching in vain for where to rest. Finding nothing but places they have already been. The Winds have power over the Earth, and every inhabitant therein. They could exact man's annihilation, were it not for the hand of God.

From beyond Olympus comes the west wind. Swiftly over the lower peaks of the Rockies, across the Black Hills, above the great ocean plains of wheat. It flows unabated to the Appalachian Range, across the mists of the Blue Ridge Mountains. Flowing gently downward, into the forests and fields of North Carolina.

The western breeze moves rapidly over the countryside, raising the dust from harvest fields. The evergreens hold steadfastly. Leaf bearers yield colors to the wind. The leaves twist and swirl towards the ground. Mixing with dusts of the land. The autumn debris blows further down east, into corn and yellow leaf tobacco country. Over and under fences and imaginary boundaries. Into the busy, cluttered lives of women and men. All who fail to hear the mournful wailing, as the wind blows through their lives without consequence. They tend to their duties, with no concern for the lonely breeze. For the centuries of longing and despair.

But there is an exception.

This, the form of a lonely Woman—

Who hears the sorrow in the cool autumn breeze.

2

I look up from my chores. Staring across the barren field behind our house. The wind becomes visible. Given substance by a swirling cloud of dust and dirt. The wind hurries across the field and into the yard. Until it blows my hair into my eyes. I wipe the black strands from my face, and return to my duties. I pick up another soaking wet item of clothing, and hang it on the clothesline.

I am 30 years old. Partly of Italian heritage, descended through my father. My long, black hair is shiny and full bodied, mostly straight, falling about my shoulders and the length of my back. Whether or not my features are what is known as perfect, I do not know—my dark brown eyes are large, and set a natural distance apart, underneath eyebrows naturally arched. My nose would likely go unnoticed—there are no glaring imperfections on its structure or form. It is neither too small nor too large, nor is it pointed, wide or narrow. My lips are pink of their own accord, unaided by makeup of any kind, as is the smooth, natural tint of my fair skin. My face is unblemished. Not a single square inch is marked or discolored. But my eyes have been touched by the curse of humanity. They are framed by pain and exhaustion, and betray the signs of great emotional trauma.

I am average height and weight, though the dark years have taken their toll. An ill fitting dress hangs over my large, pendulous bosom, that has always seemed too heavy for my frame. My waist is rather small, with a cinched, inward curve that flows outward into rounded hips. I am embarrassed by my figure, and I do my best to wear clothing loose enough to hide my shape from view.

I was a shy child and teenager, and only spoke to my mother.

But my mother had been cruel, and incredibly abusive. And the result is a fearful, reclusive woman, with a self image clouded in negativity. And locked within the remarkable expression is my most defining trait. It is a distant longing. A profound, indefinable sadness.

Perhaps that is why I hear the wind.

Its voice is heard only by those in mourning. Whose loneliness is truly epic, and greater than themselves.

The breeze swirls around me, blowing my hair and my dress. The dead leaves begin to fly down from the giant tree. A few pecans have already fallen to the ground. Soon, I will be out here in the yard with empty grain sacks, filling them with pecans for my husband to sell. I glance at the gray, furrowed bark of the huge trunk, and look up into the branches. The wind picks leaves from the tree in bunches, and flings them into the air. They drift slowly. Some falling at my feet, while others are carried away, as the wind continues its journey east. Into some other strange, lonely part of the Earth.

3

I pull the last item from the washtub. One of my husband's flannel shirts. The blue and black flannel I love to see him put on. The shirt is clean, but I can still detect my husband's scent. The smell takes my mind to him again.

I am obsessed with my husband. My body aches inside when he's gone. But when he comes home, the longing turns to apprehension. And as the sky darkens, the apprehension turns to dread.

Because it always happens after sunset.

Every bruise. Every welt.

Every drop of blood.

But I can stand the whippings. Even when the belt begins to cut into my skin. Even through blurred vision. Even when the sound of my own crying becomes muffled.

I sometimes will play a game with myself. I start at the number 100 and count backwards, once for every blow. Every so often, numbers will be left when its over. The game helps me to endure the blows. To endure the hard leather as it burns sores into my body.

Even through tears and blood, the belt is the most tolerable. Maybe, it is because my body had been prepared already. By my first tormentor. By the sticks, switches, paddles, brushes and belts that my mother had used.

The whippings are normal. I accept them as part of my life. And nearly every inch of my body bears the scars of this acceptance.

Sometimes, I'll give in to the terror of anticipation. I will break the unbearable tension, and ask him if he's going to whip me. And I hope against hope that his answer will be no. But more often than not, the answer is yes. And we will move mournfully into the bedroom and close the door.

Dressed or undressed. Quickly or slowly. Flailing or standing still. I never know what form the belt whippings will take. But when it is over, we feel better. We *both* feel better. And sometimes he comforts me afterwards. But not always. And not very often.

But there is always blood. Sometimes the blood will run, and drip from the end of a bad cut on some part of my body. These are the times when I could have started at 300, and easily counted down to the bottom. But the game doesn't always work. Sometimes the pain is too great.

Every once in a while, he hits me with the buckle.

It breaks pieces out of my skin. It leaves bloody, square shaped welts. The first time it happened, I thought I was going to drop dead from the pain. But these sessions don't last as long. He is satisfied much quicker with these.

The buckle serves as a marker. The line between what I can take, and what I cannot.

Whipping. Pinching. Knuckles to the ribs. Punching. Biting. Bondage. Hunger. Thirst. Exposure to the weather. Imprisonment. Bent fingers and toes. Twisted wrists and arms…

These, I can take. People all over have been raised on such things, and still are not sure if they were abused.

But there are things I cannot endure.

The safety pins. The jagged wooden sticks.

The ropes and the pillow.

And the nail.

It had caused my arm to be broken. Last November, just before our 9th wedding anniversary.

He made me strip down in the cold house.

The nail being dragged across my back was too much. I couldn't keep my back to him. I knew I'd get something worse if I moved. But I didn't care.

So, when all I got was swung around and slammed into the wall, I was relieved…

But then, he kicked his boot hard into my right forearm. We both heard the bone snap. I had sat on the floor, shivering and holding my swollen arm for an hour, before he helped me get dressed and took me to the emergency room.

"I fell down the stairs. I'm so clumsy. I'm always falling."

An arm cast. I was in it for six weeks.

The night after it was removed, followed the worst whipping I'd ever received. It was one we had both known was coming. The one I had dreaded. It left me nearly unconscious and covered in blood. But like all the rest it ended. And I was still alive.

For years now, things have been getting worse. More sadistic.

Two months ago, when I saw the big safety pin, I was bewildered—

"Why? Please tell me why you have to do this?"

Of course, he does not answer. He only gets behind me.

I face forward and close my eyes. I feel him grab one of my breasts, and pull it forward.

The pin is suddenly pushed into the bottom of my breast. I scream a hellish noise, like one who is burning in the Lake itself.

The pin scrapes a small cut under my left breast. The blood runs down my stomach.

He lunges at me and grabs me again. But I fight him. With every flame of this Italian fire. He can't position me again. I am too strong, and his groin aches from a well placed kick.

He stands by the bedroom door so I can't run away. But I run quickly into the bathroom and lock the door.

"I won't do it. I won't let you hurt me anymore!"

He throws the pin away. He steps back into his socks, blue jeans, and boots.

The old bathroom door won't open. With every ounce of strength he pulls it, but it will not open. So he suddenly kicks it with all his might.

I scream and climb into the bathtub.

The window is too small. I know I'll never make it. The door... the door is splitting. A few more kicks...

"I'll come out! I'll come out, now!"

He begins to grunt as he kicks. The plywood starts to splinter. Just a few more…

His foot suddenly breaks through the door, and my screaming gets deeper. They are death screams.

He reaches through the jagged, splintered hole in the door and unlatches the knob.

"I won't fight anymore! I promise! I won't fight anymore!"

With both hands, he grabs me by the hair and drags me into the bedroom. He throws me down onto the middle of the floor and puts his foot into my back. He takes hold of my right arm, pulls it up behind me, and leans forward on it with all his might.

My screams are beautiful to him. Like music. They send waves of pleasure through his body.

It won't come out. My arm won't give. So he stops leaning on it and flips me over onto my back. Put your arms to your sides, he yells.

He kicks me in the shoulder. Very hard.

I comply, but too slowly.

He kicks me again.

I close my eyes and beg God to help me. The pain burns acid under my left breast. But I wait. I wait for the pin.

But he's not concerned with the pin—

He positions himself, and brings his knee down with full force onto my left collar bone. The dull popping sound is as clear as day. The pain shoots to every part of my body.

The substance of my flesh dissipates. Reforming into blue and black fire. I scream to God and Christ, while he pins both of my arms to the floor with all his strength.

He watches as I writhe in torment. Trembling, shaking, babbling like a madwoman. I seem nearby the edge of sanity. He quickly swings around and lays on top of me.

But I can't hear him. I can't hear anything. I can only tremble and scream.

I begin to sweat, and my eyes roll in my head. The room grows darker. I can't think. I can't remember anything. The room is so dark now that I can't see.

The pain is going away. It feels wonderful.

After I pass out, he lays on me for several minutes. Listening to me breathe. He presses against the bone.

I don't move, but the bone does. He knows for sure that my left collar bone is broken.

Eventually, I wake up. He helps me get dressed, and we take another trip to the hospital. He makes me get out of the truck and go inside alone. The doctors and nurses are all different this time. I am lucky. Hardly a word needs to be spoken. I give them the same explanation about my clumsiness. And about falling down.

"Yes, I will be more careful. Thank you. Bye bye now."

The autumn wind blows again. Whirling dust into my eyes. Swirling my long, dark hair into my face.

The wind chills my body. It warns me of things to come. It tells me to flee. To run far away from this place. But I'm too afraid. And I am in love.

So I choose not to hear the wind, which warns of the sorrows of winter.

I pick up the washtub, place it on the back porch and go inside. Into a house of fear.

A house of shadows.

4

The sense of approaching evil is overwhelming.

I have to stand and pace around nervously. The radio volume is up again, but the music brings no comfort.

I am afraid—

And there it is! The sound of his truck, approaching the house! Like so many times before, the noise fills me with relief *and* nervousness. But at least he is home—that part of it is done. So I turn off the radio and, in a whirl of emotions, go out the front door to greet him.

The dim headlights hang low over the long dirt road. I watch as they float closer. The lights shine like the eyes of an approaching night demon, which has already seen me through the walls of my house.

Chris usually gets home before nightfall. I have rarely seen the lights in total darkness.

They look like eyes

Whispered prayers would just open the floodgates, and what good would that do? So I gird my emotions, and boldly step into the front yard. To rescue him from the perils of another long, hard day.

The dark, country nights have character and substance. He can barely distinguish the little house in the pitch black. As he turns into the yard, the headlights illuminate the shape and form that is his wife.

Why didn't you leave, he thinks.

Why can't you just run away?

I wait anxiously as he turns the stylish black truck around. Tonight, I need to end our separation quickly. As I hurry around the back of the truck, each step feels more difficult than the last, like running through deep mud after a rainstorm. But I fight hard through the oppressive night—as if across a great expanse—to where my husband is waiting.

Quietly, I move to the driver's door, watching as he takes the keys out of the ignition. He opens the door, then steps out in front of me.

At last, there he stands. All six feet of him. I hug him tightly, taking a rest from the night of worry.

"I'm so glad you're home."

I am too, he says. Holding me. Breathing the scent of my long hair. Like *strawberries*...

But truthfully, we are both in pain. And we are both afraid.

He was buying me a rose

A beautiful rose

When the truck door is closed, I happily grab his right arm, ignoring his pensive mood. I begin to escort him to our little house.

A dreadful whistling comes from the dark woods. A shrill, eerie call. *Wood devils,* my mother had called them.

"Those things scare me."

That owl?

"Yes."

Only mice should be afraid of them.

I'm glad I haven't mentioned the late hour. It is warm outside, but the breeze still raises goose bumps on my skin.

"You must be starving. Dinner's still on the stove. I'll fix it while you clean up, okay?"

His expression is kind. Very meek and humble. I throw him an earnest glance, fighting the urge to ask him where he's been, ignoring the exhaustion in his handsome face. I open the old screen door, as we both stop to let the other go first.

"Whoops, excuse me." Embarrassed, I hurry through the door to get out of his way. "I'll get your bath first."

Every so often, I'll walk with too much abandon. Chris tries not to watch my dress switching back and forth. He averts his eyes, while he closes the front door. He walks into the matchbox of a bedroom, tossing his keys, pocket change, wallet, and whatever else onto the little dresser.

For nearly a decade, this little country house has been our home. We are jaded to its plainness. To the spirit of misery in the walls. There is a tangible oppressiveness that affects his mood. Sometimes, it feels like the house itself is taunting him. Tugging at his emotions, to remind him of cruelties from his own past.

I am in the bathroom, running water into the tub. The sound of the water is loud in his ears. He plops down at the foot of the bed and takes off his boots and socks—socks which were once white, a long time ago. I am whistling over the noisy water. He thinks about how easy it is to tolerate my incessant whistling and humming.

Bugs Bunny—

A lively, beautiful melody he hasn't heard in years. It almost makes him feel better. Almost. As I walk past him, he notices my hair, my skin, and my lips, contorted in whistling form.

There were times before I was married, when I had been noticed. But when they got a good look at the saintly, naïve expression, they were overcome with pity rather than lust.

I might have been a good nun. But that wasn't my destiny.

I am married.

Elizabeth! What about this bathtub!

The noise of the water is driving him crazy, and the smell of the roast is making him sick.

"Just a second. I'll be right there."

Never mind, he says. I'll get it.

He finishes undressing, down to his underwear. Years of farm work and a lot of protein have done amazing things to his muscle tone, and as it was with his mother, his own beauty is considerable.

I hurry back into the room. Still tasting a bit of gravy on my fingertip.

I said I'll get it, he snaps. You can get these clothes up for me.

"Okay. I'll finish heating—" The bathroom door closes hard in my face. The lock clicks.

He's just tired and irritable

I gather up his filthy clothes, but the hamper is in the bathroom. I toss the clothes in the corner by the closet.

I'd better leave him alone

My lonely rose lays unattended on the dresser. I smile to myself, as I open the closet and take out the soft bristled shoe brush. I pick up his tan leather boots and take them outside to brush them. On the back porch, I listen to the variety of country night sounds. The noisy trill of the tree frogs blends with the crickets' melody, both supported by the low, deep *whooming* of the bullfrogs. I half expect to hear another whistle from that lonely screech owl…

But louder than all of this is the incessant splashing from the bathtub, which I can hear through the thin walls.

The Moon has moved from behind the cloud veil. As I brush the dirt from his boots, I catch a glimpse of the massive silhouette of the giant tree. The tree always reminds me of that cold January night, ages ago, when fear had sent me running outside in the snow. So I wouldn't hear. So he wouldn't know that I had gotten pregnant again.

No children

The memory causes me to take a deep breath, and steady myself against a sadness wave.

When the boots are finally clean, I go back to the bedroom. The splashing now seems louder than ever.

"Chris?"

Yeah?

"Are you gonna eat tonight?"

Just leave it out.

"Alright."

I can't ask him... I can't ask him where he's been.

"I've been keeping dinner warm for you since *six* o' clock. So it probably won't taste as good."

It'll be fine.

But like that famous, nosy cat, the curiosity gets the best of me. I move closer to the door.

"I... I really missed you tonight honey. I was worried about you." A timid voice. Full of hidden sorrow. "I was so happy when you got home that I hardly knew what to say. But I'm glad you're here now, and that you're alright."

No answer.

"Where..."

I whisper it. A cold, invisible hand tries to hold it captive...

"Where were you tonight, sweetie?"

The splashing stops.

"Chris, if there's anything wrong I'd like for us to talk about it. You can tell me anything and I'll understand."

Silence.

"I'll just wait in the kitchen. I'll see you in a minute, okay?"

I get the answer I expect. More splashing.

The wave of sadness finally hits, devastating my façade. I stroll quietly back to the kitchen, followed closely by fear and depression. While I stand in the kitchen, I feel it coming for me again. Through the open window.

A breath of *winter*.

I simply close the window. And choose not to hear the cold wind.

5

*H*e often thinks of his own mother. Cold, brutal memories. Burning through his mind and body without mercy.

His t-shirt lays across the back of the chair. He sits still, shirtless on the edge of the bed, looking at the old wooden floor. Exhaustion rules, but sleep is out of the question.

Chris had already told me he wasn't hungry. He listens as I rattle noisily about the kitchen, putting away the once in a lifetime roast and gravy. A masterpiece, reduced to leftover status.

The lights go off in the kitchen. Lonely footsteps shuffle towards the bedroom. He watches me step lightly in, glimpsing my sad expression, which I try to soften. I sigh deeply, sitting on the bed beside him.

"You about ready for bed?"

He only sighs, then rubs his face with both hands.

For nearly a decade, this little country house has been our home. We are jaded to its plainness. To the spirit of misery in the walls. There is a tangible oppressiveness that affects his mood. Sometimes, it feels like the house itself is taunting him. Tugging at his emotions, to remind him of cruelties from his own past—

"I got lucky tonight. I heard *The Barber of Seville* on the radio. Nothing from the opera, though. Just the overture. That's my favorite, you know."

A nervous pause.

"I wish they would play it more. I never get to hear Rossini."

I run my hands through his soft, brown hair. Trying a gentle, hypnotic stare.

"Don't you want to go to sleep now?"

"In a minute."

"Well, I'm gonna put my nightgown on and go to bed."

I step into the bathroom, just out of sight, and began to undress—

The classic shape, with what some might call a *country bosom*.

"Do you have to work tomorrow?"

"We got the last field cleared, so some of us are takin' a couple of days off."

"Good. I've been missing you a lot. We can spend the whole time together."

"I'm not stayin' cooped up in here."

"Oh." I am startled, and a little hurt. "Are we going somewhere?"

"*We* aren't going anywhere," he says.

His tone had changed just enough. I suddenly long for rest and sleep. To leave this day behind forever.

There are rarely any true warning signs. I cannot tell if I am feeling just a breeze, or the prelude to a storm.

I slip into my nightgown, hanging my dress in the closet.

"You need some time to yourself anyway. I'll be waiting for you. We'll eat that roast when you get back."

"Who says I'm comin' back?"

The look bores into me like an ice drill. It is as familiar as the seasons.

My heart pounds. My breath quickens. I sit down beside him, grabbing his hand and looking fearfully into that cold stare. A handsome stare.

"Chris, just tell me what's wrong," my voice trembles. "Tell me what's the matter, and I promise we can fix it."

I hold his hand tightly, caressing his face.

"Shut up and take your hands off me."

"Chris, I can't. I want you to tell me what's wrong, so we can…"

"Shut…*UP!*"

He snatches his hand away. Violently.

"Chris I'm sorry," she whispered…"I'm so sor—"

My voice chokes off, when he takes hold of my *throat*—

We both stand up slowly. Instinct locks me in a passive position. I don't touch him, and I offer no resistance. My loud, shallow breathing tells of his tightening grip.

"I shouldn't have come back," he says.

Now, I understand…

He had *abandoned* me.

But he had reversed his path. Back across the miles towards the little house. The warnings had taken form in a premonition, and a cold ghostly wind…

24

But I love him, and have chosen to endure.

"You haven't learned anything, have you?"

"Chris, I've learned it. I won't do it again, I swear to *God*—"

My chest heaves with each breath. He lets go of my throat, taking hold of my arm, guiding me through the living room to the dark kitchen.

"Chris what can I do? What can I do to make it better—"

"Shut up. And turn that light on."

I hurry across the small room, and flip on the light switch.

Run away Elizabeth

"Where's the knife?"

I creep over to the only drawer in the room, and remove a small, dull steak knife.

"Not that one."

With a trembling hand, I take from the drawer a large, black handled carving knife.

"Now put it on the stove."

As I obey him, I think of my impending mutilation. Where he will cut first. But he only stands calmly with his arms folded, leaning against the refrigerator.

"Put the blade across the burner."

My hand is shaking.

"Now turn it on. On *high.*"

I click the proper switch. The burner begins to smoke and spark, singeing away the residue that always hides out in stoves, no matter how clean they may appear.

Timidly, I move over to him, caressing his arm. My shaky, pathetic courage intrigues him. But he is unmoved.

"What sh—what should I do now?"

He spins me around hard, pushing me towards the light switch. My breath comes in fearful little gasps.

"Turn it off."

"Are you ready for bed now?" I ask, staring at the stove in the dark.

We are a controlled fire of rage—

And controlled terror.

"I'll turn off the stove… and th--and then we can go to bed, okay?"

A faint crackling sound. The coils glow a hot, bright orange in the dark. A strip of black divides it, where the eight inch knife blade rests.

"I'll… I'll t-turn off the st-stove…"

Fear. And *extreme* denial. I try to get to the stove, but he jerks me quickly backward.

"Yes, I'm ready to go to bed now…"

Wake up Elizabeth

"Y-Yes, I'm ready to go sleep, I *am* kinda tired-"

My gaze is fixed on Satan's Fire. My body trembles, as if powered by a hidden energy.

"You'll learn tonight," he says. "I *swear* it."

"Yes, I'm hungry too," my voice chokes. "I'm glad you're hungry, I'll fix the-the stove if you want can t-take it out of the st-stove, I mean, th-the refrigerator…it'll be ready in a m-minute, o-k-kay…"

With his thumb knuckle, he pushes hard into my side. A sharp, stabbing pain. I draw a breath.

"No… I mean… I've learned already…"

My side is in agony. But I know it is nothing.

I know that I am nothing.

"I…I swear, Chris. I swear to *God and Jesus* I'll never do it again. I won't nag you about where you've been. You can come and go and do whatever you want and I'll *never* bother you about it, okay? Okay, Chris?"

In the dark, he is alarmed by my expression. It bears a look of profound disbelief. A look of quiet madness.

"Undo those buttons," he orders. My fingers tremble. "Now, put your hands on that table."

He moves my long hair to the side, then yanks the gown hard from around my shoulders.

The top of my back is exposed.

My bare skin.

"And if you move," he says, "I'll make it worse than you can imagine."

"You can tell me about it C-Chris… you can always tell me about anything and we'll take c—please tell me what to do—"

These lessons are always brutal.

But this is different.

A soft, tapping noise. His finger, testing the knife handle. He takes a firm grip, lifting it off the red burner.

He loves me too much to do this—

I can hear him breathing, just behind me.

And then—

A flash of white *heat!*

"Chris!…"

A long pause.

"Chris, help me! Please!"

The old bedsprings creak. The pain hits me so hard that I grab the pillow, pulling myself forward on the bed.

"Chris!"

He jumps up and slides the kitchen table hard into the wall. The noise booms. Then silence. He knows there won't be another peep.

I will endure it, as I am accustomed to.

In pitch darkness, he slides the kitchen table back into place and sits down again. His elbows are on the table. He leans into his hands, rubbing his face and clawing at his hair. Like all madmen have done.

The midnight breeze picks up outside, and the house immediately takes on that unnatural cold that so many tell about, but don't really believe in. The darkness around him seems to come to life. He has to struggle to keep from running to the light switch like a frightened child.

The old bones of this house often creak and moan, as if something were moving among the shadows.

He listens as I start the loud, quick panting. It goes on that way until he can't listen any longer. So finally he gets up from the chair and goes to the bedroom. When he turns on the light—

"I'll be quiet! I'll be quiet! I won't make any more noise!"

I am sobbing, with a contorted, ugly expression. Tears are streaming down my face.

He cannot say a word. He just gathers the same filthy clothes he had come home in, and dresses quietly. I stare at him with watery, red eyes. While he dresses, he takes another look at the incredible thing he has done. His blood runs as cold as the house.

"Please don't leave!" A loud, wailing plea. "I promise I won't cry anymore if you'll stay!"

He gathers the rest of his things, including his boots, hurrying out of the room. He turns the light off, leaving me there in the dark.

"Chris! Come back! Please come back! I'm scared Chris. *Chris, I'm scared!*"

In the darkness, I hear the front door slam.

"Christopher *don't leave me!*"

The burn is as painful as it was fifteen minutes ago. I feel light headed, and my skin is on *fire*—a mixture of searing, bubbling and itching. Like acid has been poured onto my back.

I had been dragged, kicking and screaming into the bedroom, and was thrown onto the bed. He had straddled my hips and clamped my wrists together… and the hot blade had been pressed into my back again. Like a drowning woman I had screamed, clutching and clawing against hopelessness. Praying for the saving miracle that I knew would never come. But if there was any luck to be had, it was that the big knife had *cooled* while he dragged me to the bedroom…

On my back is a single, very large *blister*—except for a bright red sore, where the skin had been burned away. The darkened skin is puffed up around the sore, giving it a fiendishly unique appearance. As burns go it is a work of art. It would have been the talk of the entire hospital. But its origin would have been no mystery, attracting the wrong kind of attention.

Or the *right* kind.

I lay still and quiet. Listening. It sounds like he is putting his boots on outside the front door..

About a minute later, I hear his keys jangling.

The truck door opens and closes—

The engine starts.

I want to get up and run to the door. But there is too much pain. Searing, mocking pain. Somehow worse than any I've ever felt. And it won't stop. I know it isn't going to stop.

The truck drives away. I am alone in the dark…

And then I feel something, like the tip of a *finger,* touch me hard on the sole of my foot—

I scream bloody murder, jump off the bed, and run to the light switch as fast as I can.

Nothing is there.

I stand alone in the house. Trembling. Looking around. I would love to turn on the other lights, but fear awaits in shadow. To whisper from the walls. I am too afraid to go in the living room. And the kitchen is out of the question. The 23rd psalm is upon my lips.

After a minute or so, I have enough courage to walk quickly to the other rooms. All the dim lights in the house are now on. It is less fearsome. I switch on my radio, turning it up loud.

The music is just too moody. And there is no melody. So I turn away, finding a friendly voice. That is better. Now the house is not so empty. So desolate.

A new strength flows. The second wind. I am able to get myself a quick drink of water. I return to my place on the bed, this time with a Bible. I open it to John's gospel and try to read a verse or two.

Impossible. But I am content to leave it open, flipping the pages until I find one where every word is in red. Then I move it to the side and lay my head down on the pillow. But this time, my feet are facing the *opposite* direction. Towards the headboard.

The light and the voice help do the trick. Now, I am less afraid.

When he hits me, it is there.

In every corner. In every shadow—

The evil.

Something touched me. I felt it.

I'll die here soon.

The radio man's voice is soothing. A kind voice.

The voice begins to change…

A violin?

As I drift to sleep, the radio voice whines. The soft, atonal cry adopts a definite tone.

A violin.

The tone begins to sing a melody. The single violin expands, until it is many playing at once. The notes grow, until I am dreaming of a single, harmonized piece for violins alone. They are joined by violas, cellos and double basses, all merging into an extended phrase. A lilting rhythm, that burns a fiery passage. Lightly textured, and filled with the purest, most intoxicating melody.

As I have so many times before, I dream of music. My music.

Melodies resound the Great Music Hall. I find myself before a small ensemble, listening intently. These are the Players of Orchestra's Light— their sounds fill the room of a small cathedral, reverberating fully. As I stand there, I am aware of the pain in my back, but can easily endure it. I know I am seeing a three part piece in sonata form. For string orchestra.

A string sonata.

The organ is beautiful. And the window. There is a golden angel in the window. The cross is made of gold. As is the alter. The ceiling rises to infinity. The grandest echo it sings. The two ivory statues are my guardians. Are they saints? Angels?

The music is so beautiful, the echoing sound so perfect that I find the strength to endure the burning. My compensation? Maybe. But no struggling, frustrated composer would trade places with me.

The price is more than they could pay.

ome thoughts will fade
And cower from Lucid's glare
There they flourish in the dark of Shade
In the place where dreams are made

In her dining room mirror, the Lady gazes a divine reflection. Frustrated, she gathers her purse from the oakwood table, and clip-clops midnight blue heels through the kitchen, down the long hallway to her bedroom.

A masterpiece. Done entirely in shades of gray, with white and subtle, piquant touches of color. Vera tosses her blue leather purse onto the huge bed, followed by the Klein crystal timepiece, which shares with her pumps the designer's name she loves. She slips Anne's lovely shoes off to the floor, glad for plush, gray carpet at her feet. Slowly she steps over to her closet, trying not to think about Brenda and Catherine Grace Harrison. Resisting the deeper truth about what she feels. About what she deals with every single day…

It is all consuming. Keeping her buried in a mild, continuous haze. Sometimes it is severe, and it cripples her.

Thousands of land acres, and more money than anyone will ever need.

Who cares?

What is success without joy and laughter?

Vera's closet is a room unto itself. It embarrasses her that she has so many dozens of high cost dresses and purses, and nearly *seventy* pairs of shoes, only a few of which she has ever worn. In front of her closet mirror, she gladly slides out of the snug, crème colored fancy with its midnight blue flower pattern, watching her bra rise into view, noticing the sheer size of what it conceals. Slowly, she frees them from their blue lace prison, enjoying the heavy weight of them as she bends over to remove her stockings.

Privately, she relishes her body's sensitivity. The aching that churns beneath cultured civility. Her curviness is powerful to be sure, but incites little modesty. The southern church dignity has scant influence over her clothes—her skirts and dresses, shirts and jeans are uncompromising. But she can hardly admit, that she enjoys the idea that what she wears is too tight, and that her husband's workers have to avert their eyes to the sky when she comes around. She understands every part of it, though. The loveliness. The sensuality made irresistible by gray eyes and a voluptuous, curve-waisted figure.

After a long moment, she looks away from the mirror, returning her favorite crème dress to its place, draping her bosom and desire into plain house gear— hip hugging denim shorts and powder blue tee. She is glad, because she prefers her farmer's wife clothes anyway.

Now she is comfortable. Home, in her southern palace.

The house is too big—

Too empty

It would be nice to have someone to talk to. The fields were cleared weeks ago, but her husband was still working. She smiles a little, thinking of how after all the years, he still melts at her best submissive displays. When she'd got home earlier, she had sent him out of the house burning after their little kitchen game. But now she is lonely for him. How she has prayed to be rid of the paperwork! And worries about the weather, and fertilizer, and limestone, seed prices, bushels per acre, market price per bushel, pesticide, weed killer, soil ph, equipment parts and pay checks—

Briefly, her mind fades back to that soft spoken young worker. The one with the kind disposition, and the *eyes.* Every so often, she wishes he would stay around a little longer.

To talk.

Maybe, she'll ask him about his lucky wife.

Or maybe not.

It had been growing since the first day he had rung her bell, and said that John told him to come by if he wanted a job on the farm. The feeling had hit her like a cold pain. An icy wind—from the moment she opened the door. From the moment she looked into his eyes…

Lightning, it had been. So shy and polite, he was. And that face.

Aspirin taken, she leaves the private bath to itself, strolling back into her Saturday afternoon *ennui*. Cozy, spacious comfort waits for her. She feels herself floating past the dining hall, into the massive living room to the white grand, touching a key unknowingly, then over to the gray cushioned sofa, which curves from one side of the world to the other. The Lady settles down into leisure, placing her soft drink on the end table and closing her eyes. Though she tries not to let it happen, a certain *Brenda* and her famous daughter *Catherine Grace* claw their pretty selves into her memory. Out of necessity, Vera had excused herself early from their arctic breezes. Driving home alone.

Vera understood that sometimes, there is nowhere to go. No one to turn to. But most never come to terms with this. Flitting, fluttering from house to house. Pillar to post. Person to person. Collecting enough so-called friends and acquaintances to seat an auditorium. But some—even the most likeable and well to do—have made an unfortunate observation:

That there *are no connections*. Except those provided by Fate…

And that people are consistently disappointing. And that human nature often dictates cruelty and betrayal.

Vera suddenly finds herself slipping. Sliding down, drowned in waters of evening flow. In the rising—the dark'ned tide of deep depression she is lifted, gliding through the living room, adrift in sorrow to her Gray Palace.

To seek a cure for the loneliness…and the pain of living.

To sleep.

I haven't been outside since that night. I haven't cooked or cleaned or washed clothes. Chris told me not to worry about it, that he would take care of those things himself.

How very sweet of him.

The burn has completely healed. But as scars go, it is a thing of beauty—like a kind of strange and wonderful birthmark. No—

A birth*right*.

But the skin on my back is healed, and the pain is gone away. I'm out in the backyard, in the cold shadow of the giant tree. Pecans cover the whole yard. I'm busy piling them into sacks by the pound.

The day's chill is true. Not from some ghostly breeze, but from the late Autumn weather itself. The sky—a rich, deep blue, with a scattering of fluffy white clouds in the distance.

It is November. Our anniversary month.

Across a decade of seasons.

Too many pecans

Scores of them. Too many to count. I mindlessly toss them in the empty grain sacks by the handful. Lower back pain works me sore, so I raise up to stretch and take a rest. A few leaves still drift from the Flowering Tree.

A quick glance over the top of the house reveals a pleasant surprise. Far off in the distance is a cloud—

A towering, billowing mountain of light, shining bright in the afternoon sun. The cloud top glows impossibly white, revealing from within itself the smallest part of the glory of Heaven.

I'm compelled to ask Him for mercy, and the strength to endure.

But Redemption seems too far away—

So I turn away from the Light, tending my duty of survival.

I finish filling the bag and tie it up, placing it with the others near the tree trunk.

A rustling sound—

Something moving through some dead leaves. A squirrel maybe. I look, but I don't see anything.

The noisy chickens seem to call me. I wander over to their fenced in yard, watching them peck and scratch in the dirt, listening to what they have to say. I have seven white hens and one speckled one. Years ago they were all the size of my fist and bright yellow, except for my speckled one.

They hardly lay a single egg anymore. Earning their keep as little more than yard pets. Hungry little feathered diversions.

One of their companions met its fate a while back. The big, white Bantam. Its crowing had gotten on my husband's nerves for the last time. A violent, chaotic little scene with me pulling at him, screaming and begging for him to have mercy for the poor thing.

I grab a handful of feed, tossing it to the hungry chickens. For the first time in six weeks, my husband can hardly look at me. I know what that means.

Years of the unspeakable—

Thus, the fear.

But its been a long time since I've had anything to be afraid of.

Such a long time.

Chris arrived about an hour later than usual. Apparently, there had been a small errand to run. He was carrying a small bag. I never asked what was in it.

The sun has been down for some time. Chris ate the meal that I prepared him. His favorite meal—breaded pork tenderloin, with fried potatoes and onions.

After dinner, he sits at the table with a glass of sweet, homemade lemonade, reading the newspaper. I've retired to the bedroom, listening to my classical station and trying to read my Scriptures.

I've been staring at the same page for an hour.

I take a deep breath, remembering that in the past, there have been *real* reasons to be afraid. So, a conversation should be no problem. There's no need to cower in fear from a talk.

There should be nothing to fear.

I close the Bible, place it on the stand by the radio, and traverse through fear and bravery to the kitchen. I drift up behind him, gently touching his shoulder.

"Hey."

Hmm, he answers, still reading something in *The Daily Enterprise.*

"Can I sit in your lap for a minute?"

I boldly ask, pushing myself onto him, violating every inch of his personal space. I kiss his forehead and look into his eyes—those pale, azurean eyes, that still melt or freeze me every time I see them.

"You don't talk to me. You don't look at me. You don't touch me. What happened?"

No answer.

"Chris, I don't want you to leave. I'm glad you come home every day. And I don't care about your job or this old house. And it doesn't matter that we don't have anything…"

I pause.

"The only thing I care about is *you.* I want us to have a good life. I want us to live in peace."

I glance at the tiny window by the kitchen door. It is dark outside, and the house is getting colder. I take another deep breath. A deep, trembling sigh.

"I have to ask you something. Something important. Chris—I'm asking you please… *please* don't let it happen anymore."

His expression betrays his turmoil. His frustration.

I—

A pause. A fearful look at the darkness outside the window—

I'm going to make you wish you were never born.

Sometimes, a person can grow accustomed to fear. The words he spoke, their sound, burrows into my mind. The thing grows, and quickly sends cold to the rest of my body. I sit quietly as the fear spreads, until I am chilled to the bone marrow.

But I endure it, as I am accustomed to.

"Um… I'm gonna go to the bathr… I mean, the bedroom now, so you can relax—"

Did I tell you to move? he says, anguished. Did I say that you could move, or speak?

I swallow hard. "Don't think about me anymore. You just relax and finish reading your newspaper." My voice is shaking, and I'm stroking his hair, while staring at the paper. You just think about relaxing, and… okay? You just forget about me and my big mouth and my face …"

He watches me tremble and look around the room. Its as though I can see things coming out of the walls.

I'm going to get away from you now, so you can relax, okay?

I stand up, *very* slowly. But I know better than to walk away.

I know better.

Ice cold brushes my forehead, as the invisible sweat begins to evaporate. But I don't move.

"Promise me you'll think about the good things, Chris. Just promise me that, okay? Promise me?"

The cold stare. The blank, merciless expression.

I don't want to die

Please, God, don't let me die

Get away from me, he says. I turn and march quickly into the bedroom, closing the door.

Christopher stares angrily at the dark window. He is angry because there is no salvation.

No deliverance from suffering.

In the bedroom, I sit on the foot of the bed, staring at the window. But truthfully, there is nothing to see. Only darkness.

I can't cry. And there is no terror. I feel mostly numb and empty. Again I pray. Not for deliverance, but for strength.

Outside, the November wind suddenly blows hard, weeping and howling over the affairs of men. And of women. I turn on the radio, hoping to lose myself in my passion. Nothing. A piece with no melody. No inspiration. So I turn it off, and focus on my own imagination. I go back years, all the way to the beginning. I begin to remember the first pieces my mind ever gave me. Inspired little melodies for the piano. Visited in dreams, and waking visions when I was only twelve. In the dreams, I played them on a piano I had seen my music teacher play in school.

This music has been locked away in my memory. Every note is stored for when I need them. I close my eyes and begin to replay one from the beginning. But it seems trite. Too restricted, too primitive. The tight forms and structures are too confining.

My mind races the files and reserves of my most inspired passages. I return to my cathedral, and to the *fire sonata* for strings. When I hear again the rhythmic freedom, the melodic purity and inspiration, I make a solemn vow. My music will always reflect my love for pure melody. Uncluttered and unhindered by too much structure.

All of my finished pieces will be collections of treasures. Joined phrases of the most sublime melodic beauty. Structured minimally. Laid together as only they know best.

The cathedral is not as cold as the house. The evil has no power there.

The acoustics. The marvelous echo. When the chords stop, the echo sends their memory reverberating throughout.

Perfect sound.

*izabeth!*

My mind's cathedral dissolves. I find myself staring at old, gray walls. My grand overture echoes in my head, and for a moment I don't know where I am or what I am doing.

I recover from my musical trance. The beautiful beast leans in the doorway with its arms folded. Staring at me through eyes the color of ice.

There's no need to pretend you can't hear me.

"I… I can hear you." The fear spreads again.

He closes the bedroom door.

Get up.

I obey.

Take off your clothes, he says.

I unbutton the front of my old, dull white dress in tiny rose flower pattern, and let it fall to the floor. My face flushes bright red, but I only stand still, with my arms down to my sides.

At times like this, my music is silent.

Though he tries to prevent it, his eyes lower anyway, to look at my curvy, voluptuous body.

But familiarity breeds contempt. Chris easily grunts mock disapproval. I lower my eyes and begin to fidget with my hair. I want to hide. To run and hide, and be left alone. I've had enough of the fear. The cold. The humiliation…

The betrayal.

In front of me, he strips off his shirt, pants, shoes and socks. His tanned, toned body is exposed down to his underwear. The look on my face is pure dejection. A disgust for my current fate.

He walks over to the little closet, still looking at me. Watching me. In case I decide to run.

But run where?

From the back of the closet, he picks up a small length of rope that he uses to tie my wrists. And a longer piece, used to bind my legs together.

I know what to do. I turn my back to him.

There isn't a single piece of cloth over the window. We don't need any. Beyond the window is a space of grass, shadowed by a thick, dark woods. No one will ever see through the exposed window, and witness the tortures that occur in this room.

I stare at my faint image in the night window, while my husband ties my wrists behind my back.

And then, something new—

He ties the longer rope around my *neck* and to my bound arms, pulling them further up than ever. I grunt from the pain in my shoulder. I hear the belt buckle jingle. Already my body itches as it remembers the bloody welts. My breath quickens.

The soft, crinkly rasping of the plastic bag. He tosses it on the bed and steps up behind me. I brace myself for the first blow—

But it never came.

He instead hooks the belt around my thighs. The tight belt calls attention to my soft flesh and voluptuousness. Bewildered, I look back at him, as he empties the contents of the bag onto the bed. It is a small package.

The fear attacks me again, and I nearly lose my breath. The ropes seem tighter than ever.

"C-Chris…Chris, honey?"

He ignores me and dumps the steel *safety pins* onto the bed. He gathers the largest, thickest ones into a pile.

"Chr…Chris…"

My voice chokes. Tears are only a blink away.

"Chris, take the belt. Take it please. Take it and beat the skin off me but *please don't do this!*"

All of the fear and sorrow begins to escape through my voice. Through tears, my voice becomes very loud and pleading. It sends a wave of exhilaration through him. It is the thrill of fear.

He is afraid for me.

10

A voice echoes in the Lady's mind. A voice from the evening.

Vera takes off her glasses. No more pretending to care about the papers on the table. The glasses take on a sudden, heavy inessentiality; why does she insist on wearing them? She folds them up, deciding it is the last time.

Grain.

She sometimes has nightmares of being swallowed alive in a grain bin. Its time to get up from here. To get out of this kitchen. Maybe she'll take a walk. A walk up to those accursed bins.

To see an angel.

The silver storage bins look a lot smaller from the house. They are a good distance away, but close enough to be easily walked to.

Vera slips on a light weather jacket and steps outside. The day is bright and sunny, and there is no breeze. It is one of those rare days, where not a single cloud is in sight, and the sky is in full, deep blue all the way to the ground. A perfect day for a walk. She begins her trip up the gravel road towards her husband, fully prepared to embarrass him by showing up around his workers again. Her light coat is short, and hides nothing of the shapeliness her jeans reveal.

Vera listens to her feet crunch into the gravel as she walks. The road seems so much wider than the last time. It is because the fields are empty. Everything looks bigger when the corn is gone. Placidly, she gazes across the barren field, beyond the sea of cropsoil. An infinite, lifeless world. An ocean of dirt, yielding its promised pot of gold.

Suddenly, a monstrous engine thunders. It irritates her, and she rolls her eyes, not bothering to look. She only steps to the side, to the edge of the dirt ocean. But she remembers her courtesy, glancing in time to catch a smile and a wave from the truck drivers. The metallic monsters roar down the road. They must be new. Both are shiny, with long, open trailers of metallic silver, with a midnight blue logo painted on. The cabs are the same blue color, with the logo in silver on the doors.

Nice. But not for long.

The grain will ruin them.

Vera stops suddenly. Halfway between the bins and the house. She stands in the middle of a vast wasteland, wondering which way she should go. But the place she came from seems too far away. Her pained expression shows the anguish, the stress of deep, heavy thinking. She doesn't know why, but she has to keep walking.

Sometimes, Vera wonders if she is losing her mind. But she takes solace, knowing that she probably isn't the first woman who's had her mind twisted by him. But why does she feel so strange about it?

She needs to talk to him.

She can't go on unless she does.

A few minutes later, she approaches the work site. John has his back to her, chatting feverishly to both truck drivers about one thing or another. Two of John's workers are at the door of the first grain bin, making sure the grain keeps coming. The yellow corn moves from a door at the bottom, up a silver gray loading arm, and is pouring into the truck.

Watching the other bin is Joe Little.

Where is he? I don't—

Oh, my.

Stepping out from the back of one of the trucks is the object of her foolishness.

To die for.

11

*V*era's heart is aflutter.

She notices that he seems very interested in the truck. Studying every inch of it while the grain pours in. Joe suddenly tugs at his jacket, motioning towards her.

His wife must have cried when he proposed

Shyness creeps in, until she is too uncomfortable to look anymore. Her attention goes to her husband, who is talking so much that he hasn't noticed her.

A simple greeting, she needed. Two seconds of up close eye contact. Anything. If only Joe Little wasn't around here today. How many times was she going to have to ask John to fire him?

She waves to the old tobacco farmer, who seems to spend about as much time here as he does on his own little farm. Ben Gregory is one of many local, old-time tobacco farmers, earning money in the shadow of these Evans storage bins. Eating their words of warning. She grins her happy church girl smile, waving to his young co-worker. Together they make a curious pair—the elder and younger versions of the same, hopeless floundering through life.

She steps back onto the road. Moving as on a current, floating past the shiny trucks. Vera cuts a fleeting glance down the row of giant silver cylinders, all shining in the bright afternoon sunlight. In trust, they hold the tens of thousands of bushels. The Evans livelihood. If John had been an Iowa or Nebraska farmer, he would have been one of the biggest, with tall, monster grain silos. But these have done fine here. All winter long, the Seven Sisters will share portions of their gold harvest. Penuriously.

Vera moves leisurely around the second truck. She takes a deep breath, preparing for Joe's filthy looks, and for what she does best—formal greeting. She thinks that maybe, her coyness is the main catalyst for Joe's disrespect. He might stop it if she didn't act so cutesy around him. In light makeup over smooth, fair skin, and blonde hair stylishly pinned, she strolls as casually as she can. Trying her best to look like the bored lady of the manor.

Is it that far from the truth?

"Ms. Evans," Joe says. Politely.

"Afternoon, Joseph."

And there he is.

Looking at her.

Waiting.

"Hello, Chris."

"Maam," he says, nodding once.

Lightning.

Vera's hand goes immediately to her hair. She couldn't help it. Her church dignity had abandoned her.

"It's such a beautiful day," she says, "I just thought I'd come out here and bother you all for a few minutes." A big, giggly smile is trying to break through.

Joe looks at them, cutting his glance back and forth between them. Sparks are flying. In quiet frustration, he mopes away.

Vera pounces the opportunity like a she-leopard.

"Chris, you look so familiar to me. Have you got family around here?"

"No maam. Its just me and my wife."

"Oh, really? How long have you two been married?"

"About ten years now."

"You should bring her around sometime, I'd like to meet her."

It was so forced, it was making her sick.

"Well, I would," he says, "but she's so shy. She's scared to death of meeting anybody."

He smiles, cheek dimpling just so. His eyes bear a cerulean sky.

"That's too bad," she says. "Maybe you can talk her into it."

"I'll probably drag her out here one day," he says. "I guess it won't kill her to wave at you from the truck."

Now, Vera

"You know, I've seen you go to your truck and eat lunch all by yourself. You should come up to the house and eat with us sometime."

"Thank you, Maam. I'll remember that."

Vera glances away casually, watching the yellow grain fall into the truck. She wants to keep talking. About the weather, the corn, his wife, his future plans, what the stores from here to Charlotte to Charleston have done to her closet, that pretty green beetle she saw on the road...about anything.

But it is time to go.

"Well, I wish I could stay and chat, but I've pestered you enough."

"You've been good company," he says.

They make good eye contact. She thinks that maybe, by some miracle, there is a small chance that he knows. That he understood.

"You ain't leavin' yet, are you?" says Joe, sneaking back in.

"I've got some work of my own I need to finish," she replies. "I've put it off long enough. I'll see you later, okay?" She touches them on the arm, and walks away. They both disturb her mind all the time. For different reasons.

Chris stares after her.

"You too, huh?" Joe asks, keeping his gaze locked on her figure as she walks. "I'd take a piece of her if I could."

Chris shakes his head. Judgingly. Wondering what Joe would do if he got a look at a certain somebody.

A certain someone.

12

When are you going to do it?

I don't know.

Well, you'd better before she runs away.

She's too stupid to run.

I know, Mother says. There's something about her… she's weak. She's pathetic. She makes you want to kill her, doesn't she?

Dreams.

Vivid echoes. Traces of the past and future. Sometimes clearer than what we see, hear and think when we're awake. Sometimes a warning. This is what I thought as I cooked breakfast early this morning. Last night's dream may have been a wake up call. It had revealed phantom voices from the kitchen… that of my husband, and of a woman I have not seen in over ten years.

The signs are everywhere. Even in his own words. Especially yesterday at sunset, in the middle of the vast, open field behind our house.

Look around, he says. What do you see?

"I… I see the trees, and--"

It starts with an 'n' .

I look around. I see North. But I don't say it.

"I don't see anything that starts with—"

What's that?"

"I said, I don't see anything—"

He puts his fingers to my mouth. Gently.

If you don't see anything, he says, then you see…

I close my eyes. A pitiful little student, I am. I am.

"Nothing?"

He stares directly at me.

Now look around you, he says. What do you see?

"Nothing."

That's what you are, he hisses quietly. That's what your life has become.

My mother's own words, coming from his mouth. Of course, a tear runs down my face.

My heart is broken.

The orange sun looks so small. So far away. The space seems to devour us. We are tiny. Unimportant. Only two of many, walking in sorrow. Towards the end of our life.

Who do you see?

"Nobody."

That's who'll be there to help you, when it finally happens. When its finally over and done with.

For many seconds, I freeze in his stare. And then his hand leaps to my long, black hair. The fear slices me like sharp, icy needles. I brace for the twisted wrist, or the punch in the stomach. As usual, the afternoon crows and ravens are noisy.

But he only holds his hand still, hardly pulling at all. He watches me. Daring me to even pretend I'm not afraid. To him, it seems that my body buzzes with pure terror. It does. I can feel it—an aura of misery around us both—the energy of hatred, violence, and fear. If we had been in the bedroom, he would have put his hand over my nose and mouth until I turned blue.

Sometimes, I wonder why there can be no end to suffering.

You know what's gonna happen in that bedroom tonight, don't you?

Through tears, I answer him. The phantom itching on my skin has already started. The tiny pin marks are starting to burn.

Get in that house.

I turn and step clumsily over the uneven cropsoil. Making it to the backyard without falling. Walking quickly to the house.

If I had looked back, I might have seen him looking away. Compassion had torn through his heart. Causing him to hurt inside.

I remember this bizarre scene from yesterday, as I prepare breakfast. It affects me even more than the tiny chips of flesh that were whipped from my skin last night. I had woke up in the middle of the night, and thought I heard him sobbing in the kitchen. While I lay in bed, wondering how much blood had gotten on my nightgown while I slept.

The wounds will heal. They always do—

But its time for a rendezvous with Logic.

I hear the springs creaking in the bed. I am glad he is going to work today. So he won't be here to stop me.

I'll do it today

Do what?

Leave?

Run?

Escape?

Scared to death to leave the yard. And even more terrified of people.

I take the rest of the ham out of the frying pan. I've suddenly lost my appetite.

Is that food ready yet?

His voice startles me. "Um… in a minute, honey. Do you want eggs?"

Go ahead and cook 'em, he says. Did you cook any bacon?

"No."

I don't want ham, he says. Cook bacon.

"Okay."

Modern, New World women. Most would slam the pan into the sink, and say…*Have you finally lost your mind?* They would have complained or cursed, or called him every bastard and son-of-a-bitch in the book until he apologized, and then served *her* breakfast.

But I am true to form. Pushing forward. Honoring that strange code of loyalty, that binds some women to their husbands' whim, will and desire. Just another curse of mankind, in a mile long list of them. I push forward.

Through the sore skin and muscles. Through the whipped and broken spirit. I have the nature of a loyal servant, who knows her place.

What would his reaction be, if I showed some backbone? What would be the result? A *broken* backbone, maybe. The last time I stood up to him, I wound up in an arm cast.

No. This isn't the place for spine or backbone. But today, perhaps the strength of endurance is gone.

Every person is afraid to die. There are some who claim not to be.

They call it courage.

That kind of courage is insanity.

Our goodbye was different this morning. Tense. I had stood at the window, watching him drive off. There had been too much guilt. Too much fear.

I do the dishes. I sweep the old floors, make the bed and clean the bathroom. All of his clothes are done, except for one shirt, a few socks and a t-shirt. Maybe I should wash them anyway... the chickens need to be fed... there are too many dead leaves in the back yard... a couple of my dresses could use a good scrubbing... there are new melodies to write... that's a beautiful piece on the radio...

I am stalling. Ferociously.

But it is time to leave.

I ignore the aches and pains, as I stuff the last of my dresses, skirts, and underwear into the old travel bag. I take my hairclips and pins, my toothbrush, shampoo, hairbrush, my blow dryer, my gray slippers, and the most important thing of all. A few of my *little notebooks*, and my pencils and pens.

I tear a piece of paper out of one of my notebooks, where I scribble my music. In them are thousands of little black dots. Little markings that display the colors I hear. Brilliant, fascinating neoclassical gems I have found, in every form. Richly textured, symphonic quartets and sonatas. Grand concertos for orchestra, with solo instruments of all kinds. Scores of fragmented, incomplete bursts of *extreme* inspiration, waiting to be finished and polished someday, so much of it in the manner of my Crown Prince. My Italian Mozart. My Swan of Pesaro.

But my notations are odd. Unique. A trained eye might dismiss the marks as the scribblings of a madwoman.

But what glorious madness. Such beautiful insanity!

> *To my beloved husband,*
>
> *Please forgive me, for the years of pain I caused you. I have to go, only because I'm too frightened to stay. But please don't be angry with me. Don't be sad. Be happy, because neither of us will have to hurt anymore.*
>
> *Christopher. My darling Christopher Peele. I love you with all of my heart. I will love you always and forever.*
>
> *Elizabeth*

13

*T*he North Carolina weather is its normal, strange self. The dead trees are the only way to tell this December morning from one in April.

I have to go now, or I won't go at all.

So, in sorrow and exhilaration, the farm girl walks down the long dirt road. Away from the Great Flowering Tree. Away from the House of Shadow. I plan to take the paved road, and walk the few miles to the little country store.

Fear has overcome Loyalty, and Perseverance. It is time to go. I can't even blame him, though I have never provoked him. Not once.

But it is time to leave.

Or at least, time to try.

Scared to death of people. Scared to leave the yard.

Apprehension.

You're all alone out here. Among the wolves.

What do you think they'll do to you, when they get their hands on you?

A noise! Something moving in the tall grass.

Dread.

I can't breathe—

Go home, Country Carmen!

Fear.

Why am I doing this?

I think I'm bleeding—

Panic.

My heart races. My mouth is dry. I am out of breath. I begin to sweat like I've been running for miles.

I turn and begin to walk back. Slowly. Carefully. As if walking away from that famous German Shepherd everyone remembers from their childhood.

A few more steps, and I'll run. Like a Mediterranean whirlwind.

I tuck the bag close to my body. There is no sound. Even the birds are quiet. But in my mind...

The truck.

Run, Elizabeth!

I run! As fast as my black leg stockings will carry me. Every tree is suddenly alive with screeching and a whistling wind. The sun is twice as large and bright as before. The road seems to stretch on forever, and my legs feel like they've been hollowed out and filled with iron ore.

And the truck is getting closer.

I have to get to the house. To the safety of the bedroom. I run like a clumsy breeze, so fast that I lose my balance and slam hard into the dirt road. I can taste the dust in my mouth, and my hands have been scraped terribly. But I get up and keep running, through a blurry, confusing world, until I am finally in the yard. Miraculously, I make it up the steps without falling, and I break through the front door and slam it behind me.

I stand in the safety of my cottage, peering out the window—panting, whimpering from pure exhaustion. My face is stained with dust, and I can hear a strong breeze blowing and the sound of his truck still coming down the road—

But there is no breeze. And my husband's truck is parked miles away, near the Evans' field.

The letter—

I hurry into the kitchen, grab the note and stuff it in my mouth. Then I hurry to the bathroom, toss it into the water and flush it away.

The coat is hot and itchy. My scraped hands are starting to burn, and I'm still having trouble catching my breath.

Still wearing the coat, and clutching the bag, I stare at myself in the bathroom mirror. It is as though I am looking at some other dirty, pathetic creature, leering at me through big, fish eyes from behind the mirror. The light is off, and it is dark. Daytime dark.

Demons—

They live inside mirrors. They can invade a reflection and stare back. That's why reflections often look so strange. So familiar, but so different.

I take off my coat, which is stained with dust, then take my things out of the bag and put everything away. Quietly, I take my place in the cushioned

64

armchair and turn on the radio, refusing to feel the red scrapes on my hands. They burn and itch, but I don't care.

It is nothing.

14

"*T*told you, didn't I?"

"You didn't tell me anything—"

"I asked you about a hundred times why you didn't fire him," Vera says. "How dense do you have to be, John?"

Vera is leaning against the kitchen counter, with her arms folded. John had made the mistake of telling her that Joe Little didn't come to work.

"Every time I ask you what your problem is with him, you just ignore me," John says. "Now I'm gonna ask you again, Vera, what's your problem with Joe Little?"

"Look, just leave me out of it," she says. "I know you promised Louise that you would look out for him, but what else is he gonna have to do before you realize he's trouble?"

"So he didn't show up to work today," John says. "What's the big deal? He's not the only one that's missed a day of work."

"He misses work. He slacks off all the time. And you just keep payin' him and pattin' him on the back. If it were anybody else you would have thrown him out of here *months* ago. And what he did to poor Ben that time a while back. I still can't believe it."

"Ben can get a little mouthy sometimes, Vera. I've seen it."

"And its not just the work, John. I… I don't trust him. He gives me the creeps."

"What?"

"Well, just look at the way he acts."

"He's a nice enough kid, Vera. You just need to get to know him a little better."

"I know him well enough already," she says. "Well enough to know he's a problem we don't need. Remember when you trusted him to take care of that harvester?"

"You just won't leave that alone will, you?"

"Just tell me what happened."

"Vera…"

"When the thing broke down, you didn't have the parts you needed to fix it, and it put you behind schedule, that's what."

John just shakes his head. It really wasn't that big a deal.

"You sure never had any problems with Chris Peele have you?" she says.

What's in a name?

A cold, electric power. One that flows into John's body and squeezes his heart. Making him regret the day those eyes walked onto his farm.

"Well, Chris is different," he says. "And he's ten years older than Joe. Of *course* I've never had any problems from him."

Yet.

"You darned right he's different," she says. "When's the last time *he* missed work?"

"So what's your point?" John's look hardens.

"Just thought I'd remind you of what a *good* worker looks like. Maybe he'll help you realize how slack Joe is, and how long ago you should have fired him."

"Look, you just let me worry about the hirin' and the firin', and tend to your own business."

Vera cut him a look.

Such a look.

"*My* business?"

At that moment the phone rings. They stand still, staring through three rings before she decides to answer it. She picks up the phone after the fourth ring, and John glares at her, before gladly taking his cue and walking out the door.

"Hello? Oh, hello Brenda. Fine, honey how about yourself. Good."

A long pause.

"Hospice? This coming weekend? Well, I suppose I could. Oh she is? *Kate*'s going to work with us?"

She pauses. Nervously.

"Oh, no. Oh, darn it. Brenda I just remembered that John wants me here this weekend. Well, he's got a lot of papers to go over, honey, and he needs me to help him. Yes, I know, and I am sorry. Well, it's just paperwork, a whole weekend's worth, you know how that is. And I was really looking forward to seeing *Kate*, too."

Miss Amazing Grace

"Well, don't yell at me honey, I just forgot… Of course I'm not trying to back out of it, you know better than that. Okay. And I am sorry that I can't make it. Alright. Love you, too, sweetie. Bye bye now."

Brenda's volunteer brigade. Vera had escaped another long weekend trapped with Amazing Grace Harrison and her mother, the Volunteer Queen of Martin County.

She needs to get a revolving door on her living room… just go, go, go, all the time.

All of this do-goody posturing—

I'm sick of it.

She suddenly remembers her husband, and how he had sneaked away from the battlefront. In her heart, she knew that every grain of corn he ever pulled out of the ground was as much hers as it was his. Sometimes, she prays that he'll have the nerve, the stupidity, to challenge her about it.

It is lunchtime, but she isn't really hungry. She often doesn't eat a single thing all day. She likes to save her appetite until dinner, which she loves. Her appetites can often be very unladylike.

She suddenly feels the need to take a walk. A nice, leisurely walk.

Vera goes over to the kitchen window. Down the gravel road, the grain bins loom like silver monsters approaching. But still a long ways off, giving the condemned false hope.

Oh my goodness

Oh my dear Lord

Vera's heart doesn't skip a beat. It *stops*, waits, and starts back up again. She isn't sure, but she thinks she feels a cold sensation run through her chest and down her left arm to her fingers. She notices that she is trembling.

Vera watches Chris the entire time he walks, until he begins to cross the big lawn towards his truck. Then she *runs* to her dining room window, so she can get a better look.

Whenever she watches him, the conclusion is always the same.

Vera takes what may be the longest, deepest breath of her life. In her little framed mirror on the dining room wall, the Lady gazes her reflection, divine, checking her face and pretty pinned up hair. In a nervous haze, she hurries back through the kitchen and out the back door.

To talk.

15

Thoughts of escape have vanished with the daylight. There's nothing to do now but wait.

And there it is!

The sound of the truck!

I should have run. I could have escaped. But the world has closed in on me again.

The truck is getting closer.

Hide…hide in the woods until tomorrow…

I shake my head, trying to clear my mind of such thoughts. I shrug off the fear, get up, and go to the front door.

Eyes—

The truck lights look like eyes in the evening.

I watch the truck turn into the yard. I choose to push through the veil, the gray covering of fear and dread. I will reach out to him from the depths of my own love and misery, until I touch the part of his soul that loves me.

Chris turns off the engine and steps out. In the next moment, he is in the arms of his loving wife.

I press hard against him, breathing in the scent of the grain dust, feeling the rough denim jacket against my face. Neither of us speak. We just stand by the truck, hugging in the shadow of the coming night. The two of us reach into our past, to a time when we had wandered in loneliness. We remember when we had found one another, and were rescued from a life of despair...

But we are both prisoners of a dark future, prophesied from the mouths of the women who gave us life.

Often enough, words of importance will go unsaid, because of fear. Fear of the response the words will produce. A response that might cause the speaker great internal pain. But pain is something I am accustomed to.

Why then, should I be afraid to speak?

"I'm afraid to go inside, Chris."

He holds me close. Staring fearfully at the dreary silhouette of our house.

"Why do we have to go in?"

"We don't have anywhere else to go."

Together, we slowly drift the cold, late Autumn evening. The world seems poised on the edge of a long, dreary winter.

I want to cry.

But the tears won't come.

16

The temperature inside is like winter. The dim lights and dull fire provide no comfort. From outside, the flickering glow from the bare windows is eerie, glowing with a dark, unnatural hue.

In only a few hours, the temperature has plunged. We stand nearby our first fire of the season. The room is alive with the dancing light from the flames, while our shadows stretch and writhe out from where we stand, playing a grisly game on the opposite wall.

The old bones of this house often creak and moan. As though something were moving among the shadows.

"You notice how cold it always is in here? Its like that even in the summer sometimes."

I pause, noticing the flames burning in his eyes.

"How was work today? Did you have any problems with Joe?"

He only sighs, and stares into the fire.

"I miss you when you're not here."

He doesn't know what he is going to say. The words come out on their own.

You're gonna *die* tonight.

The types of fear are many, and are uniquely distinguished. Among these is the Fear of Death.

"Wha...what did you say?"

No answer.

"Chris, you don't ever have to say that. You don't *ever* have to. You know how we feel about each other..."

Shut up, he says calmly. I don't want to hear that.

"Wha... what are you going to do?" My pitiful attempt to be calm is heartbreaking.

You'll find out soon enough.

"Chris, I just want to know why. If things happened to you before you met me, then just *tell* me about it. I know you don't really want to hurt me anyway, I can see it. You love me don't you? Chris, answer me. You still love me don't you, like you did when we first met?"

I step close and put my arms around his waist, still staring in his eyes. The tears I had wanted are on the way.

"You don't tell me anymore. Even when we're together in bed, you don't say it. You used to tell me all the time."

Fear flows through me, like a river of misery.

"Are you going to let this happen again?"

Mournful frustration. Tears suddenly well up in my eyes and pour down my face. I lean my forehead against his chest and begin to cry. Like a baby.

"I don't want anymore," I sob quietly. "I don't want anymore pain, Chris."

"I'm gonna cut you into little pieces."

"Don't say that, Chris!" Don't say things like that anymore!" I scream the words in anger."Chris I know you don't want to do this anymore. I know you don't want to hurt me!"

Come in the bedroom with me, he says calmly.

"No! Chris I don't want to! I want you to stop hurting me!"

I won't be able to hurt you, after tonight. Now let's go.

"No, I *won't!"* I begin to pull away.

Let's go, he says. His ghoulish patience is dwindling.

"I can't Chris! I don't want to *die!"*

I scream in fear and frustration, pulling hard against him. He can't stay calm and pull me at the same time. I have become hysterical. My fear has transformed itself.

I am *angry—*

I resist violently. But eventually he gets a good hold of me. He lifts me up, slamming me high and hard against the living room wall.

But he is in for a fight.

I go into a rage. Thrashing wildly and clawing at his eyes. But I have no claws to make his face bleed. A devoted nail biter, who doesn't have enough nails left to scratch an itch. So I clench my fist and give it to him good across his nose.

A flash of light, and a sharp pain shoots to the back of his head. His anger flares. He lights into me as if he were fighting a man. Backing off, he pushes me hard against the wall, hitting me with quick punches to the ribs. Immediately I drop to one knee. He is about to crack me good across the mouth when he remembers something—

I want her conscious… I want her to see and feel every bit of it…

Get up, he says, challenging me. You wanna fight, *get up* then!

I look tough to him at this moment. He knows that if I could have fought, I would have. Truthfully, I *am* tough. Years of gut punches has seen to that. He has to hit me *very* hard to bend me so completely. I spit onto the floor and gather my breath like an old pro.

And then, I look up at him.

In my eyes, he sees something that rekindles his rage. Something that suddenly makes him glad this is happening.

The *Satisfaction of Perseverance*—

That *I survived the best you got, and I'm still here* look…that *whatchu gon' do now, boy?* look. If I had the skill, I would beat him to within an inch of his miserable life.

He grabs me by the dress collar, slamming me against the wall. My brain rattles around in my head, and for a second, I forget who I am.

Where is the fear in my expression? The pleading terror? Perhaps, I am no longer afraid. Maybe, I am ready to die. Like a good soldier in battle.

No.

I am angry, because the person I love won't stop hurting me. Because he won't stop making me afraid.

A warm, red tickling appears in his nose. It spreads downward onto his face, just above his mouth.

Blood.

He is almost proud of me.

Get in that bedroom, or I'm gonna start breakin' your fingers. One at a time.

I stand there, somewhere between defiance and obedience. But when he reaches out to my hand, I am suddenly alert again.

"*I'll go, Chris!*" I yell, still frustrated. "I'll go!" I turn and step reluctantly through the gates of Hell. But the gates aren't closed. Not yet.

As he follows me through, his mind flashes to the rich farmer's wife, and how terribly hurt she would be.

"Chris…"

He starts taking off his shirt.

"I want us to *live.* I want to us be happy! I don't want it to be like this anymore. I don't want it to end like this!"

He pulls off his black collar shirt, dropping it onto the floor. He wears a white t-shirt underneath.

"Talk to me, Chris. Please, *talk to me!*" My stomach is aching from those punches. I have a splitting headache.

As calmly as can be imagined, he takes out his black pocket knife and tosses it onto the bed. Then, he steps over to the closet.

"*I love you.*"

The words penetrate his skin, making his body cold. But it is time for it to be over. And when I am dead, he is going to change his bloody clothes, and buy the pills he needs to do the trick.

This prevailing spirit of death, that has haunted us from the day we moved in this house is precisely why he had never bought a gun. Not for hunting, nor protection, nor target practice. If he had owned a gun, the two of us would have died ten years ago. But no such luck. We are in a cycle of rage and fear, controlled by forces we cannot understand. We are both going to suffer, until the spirit of misery is sent away.

Run, Elizabeth!

The warning reverberates, as he reaches into the closet. At first, I don't move. But then, he tosses the first length of rope out onto the floor.

Run!

Something happens inside me. My mind and body collaborate on their own, and force me to take the first step towards escape.

I run!

I am the embodiment of every flight from ghosts, evil spirits, dangerous animals and wicked men. The survival instinct kicks in. With the outstretched arms of one who seeks the bosom of paradise, I burst from the bedroom, running clumsily through the kitchen and out the back door.

izabeth!

The December evening is cold. And quiet.

I saw her run in these woods. Where is she?

Elizabeth *Peele!*

His voice carries around the tree trunks, and through the bare branches and shrubs. There is no moon to light his way through the thick, dark woods. Only the crackling of his footsteps on the dead leaf carpet tells of his whereabouts. The sound is clear, carrying easily through the still, night air.

The sound travels the short distance from his feet, to where his wife sits behind a good sized tree, huddled in terror.

Don't breathe…don't make a sound…

I had run out the back door, across the dirt road into the thick autumn woods. My arms and legs now bear half a dozen scratches to go with the scrapes on her hands. But it is better than being cut to ribbons with a sharp knife.

It is over. I'll hide until tomorrow, then try to run away again.

Fear *can* conquer Love.

It can destroy it.

Elizabeth, he whispers.

My heart is pounding so hard that I think I might have a heart attack.

The rustling footsteps are closer…

Every crackle of leaves is closer to where I sit. I close my eyes and hold my breath, as the last footstep sounds beside the tree.

Silence…

Not a sound in Creation…

Then a rough *hand* clamps hard over my mouth, muffling the scream in my throat. My head is pinned to the scaly tree bark, and my body freezes instantly from the inside out.

He grabs my head with both hands, pulling me easily to me feet. He presses his body hard against mine, still covering my mouth, squeezing my head in his grip.

The tree bark digs into my back. I smell the grain on his skin. The rage trembles his body.

"Fight me now, *witch*."

His nose is sore. A small trickle of blood has come back. He squeezes my head harder, enough to make me give a muffled cry.

I want to break every bone in your body, he says. I want to beat you until the *piss* and blood run down your leg.

The craving is one with him. Right here, he wants to beat me 'til I am unconscious, and then choke me when I wake up.

But tonight is for cutting…

He swings me around in the dark woods like a raggedy doll, as if he were trying to break my neck. Then he wraps his arms around my waist, and slams his body on top of mine to the ground. My body makes a sickening, hollow thump as it hits the forest floor.

The pain makes me think my back is broken. He ignores the pain slicing through his own wrist and holds onto me tightly, pressing down on me, making it harder for me to catch my breath.

He hates me

He wants to bite the blood out of me. Instead he spits in my face, easing up a little until I can breathe. But my struggle for air, and the fear in my eyes from having the wind knocked out of me is terrifying.

Strawberries…

The delicious odor from my shampoo. He had smelled it before, when he was a few feet away from me.

"I love you…"

A whisper, which seems to echo across the whole countryside. And now his anger, the rage, is mixed with regret. Being outside, away from the sight of that house, makes him believe he wants me to live.

He gets up and snatches me to my feet. He trudges to the edge of the woods, pulling me roughly along. I stumble after him coughing, in breathless pain and shock, but still afraid he is going to slice me open like a fish. A Carmen fish.

"Chris, you're not going to do it now are you, huh? Huh, Chris?"

The grip on my arm tightens. Strange, operatic chords play all around me. We finally make it out of the dead Autumn woods, crossing the dirt road and the yard, and through the back door.

"Chris, don't," I pant. "Just let me live so I can help you. Please let me help you."

I begin to cry again, too weak for any more hysterics. He guides me calmly through the cold house, the algid isolation, until we are again in the bedroom. He does not speak as he closes the door, glowering at me.

"You don't really hate me," I order. "It's this *house.* Its this ugly house. It's making you do these things, Chris, I *know* it. It's not supposed to be like this."

He ushers me to the bed.

"We'll move. We'll move away from this filth. We'll go to a better place, Chris, listen to me. Just let me live so I can take care of you. You don't even have to talk to me. I won't talk to you anymore if you don't want me to."

He reaches over and picks up the knife.

"*Christopher!*" I begin to back away. Chris watches my face, as it begins to contort with terror and hopelessness. Mysterious harmonies thunder. Deadly rhythms twitch.

"Chris… *please,* please don't do it!"

I back up against the door and begin to fumble with the knob.

"Chris *don't…*"

He touches the knife to my stomach, and I *yip* like a frightened dog. A single, lightning chord flashes in my brain.

Come over to the bed.

"*No...*"

Pure terror surrounds me. A palpable energy, like an electric field. He wonders how my body can survive these emotional extremes.

He places the knife tip at my throat, while I repeat over and over that I love him. He then grabs my arm, and begins to pull me to the bed.

But I can't struggle, because of the knife. I can't pull away, because he might push it into my neck.

We inch slowly. Closer to the bed.

Get on the bed.

"No...no..."

Get on the bed, or I'm gonna put you there myself!

"I can't!" My eyes are as wide open as they can get. My nose is running. My face is gray from forest dirt. I look like I've been working in the harvest field.

He grabs my hair, pulling me downward, slowly onto the bed.

"Please... please..."

As quick as a flash, he jumps on top of me. I scream as if I am being sliced open. My eyes glisten a frightening lucidity. Melodies shriek from the walls.

I'm gonna cut you, he says.

"No!"

Yes.

He tosses the knife to the side and flips me onto my stomach. He straddles my back, facing my legs and watching me thrash and kick like a trapped wild animal.

Screaming. Begging to deaf ears. He pulls my dress up, exposing the back of my bare legs.

If you're going to do it, do it now—

Without hesitation, he picks up the sharp little knife…

And he plunges it into the back of my leg.

Through this supernatural cold travels her hopeless scream. Through the decrepit glass and wood it flew, until the sound was in the December Night, witnessed by none except the Darkness, and the branches of the Great Flowering Tree.

Once, there was Love.

Strong enough to cause pain.

Tonight, there is the pain of Fear and rage—

And Cutting.

*T*he Lady sits comfortably in her bed, admiring the crystal and porcelain figures on the dresser, and the watercolor portraits, framed and spaced perfectly about the walls of her *Gray Palace*. The hazy, amorphous world of watercolors. The style can hide a multitude of sins, effectively disguising lack of vision in a work. Something like this runs through Vera's mind, as she struggles with the notion of daughters, and whether or not to ask her husband about a certain worker of his.

Viv, when are you gonna turn that light off?

She is reading the same chapter she could have finished a half hour ago. A chapter in that immortal parable of a dustbowl family, and how they endeavored to persevere. Sometimes, things weigh so heavy on her own mind, she thinks she'd like to write about them. But then she reads the author's appointed genius, and dismisses her notions as pure foolishness.

Though she tries to block them, images of her so-called best friend and her famous daughter scratch their pretty selves into her mind again. It is time to face the truth. Her friendships aren't worth the bother anymore. Empty. Phony. Years of unspoken pettiness. A river of jealousies with swirling, secret contempt. Had it really been her imagination that at their last meeting, Brenda and her daughter had ganged up on her sweetly, subtly, until it felt like she had walked into a swarm of bees? Vera remembers how angry she had gotten with herself, when she realized they had succeeded in making her want to cry.

Every so often, she wishes that Chris Peele would stay around a little longer.

To talk.

But she couldn't have stayed with him any longer today. How would it have looked? Even so, she can't ignore the feelings either. A tugging at her emotions, that he needs to talk to her again.

Dinner with him might be a nice thing. Or maybe an invitation to church. But why? One look at him and they would know. She imagines Brenda and the others, whispering about her. Everywhere she went in this town, she would feel their eyes. Glaring at her. The way they had at poor Ms. Lilly Outerbridge, after her *married* boyfriend had died in her house. Vera had always admired her bravery, for showing herself in public after that.

"John, you've got some deliveries tomorrow don't you?"

No answer.

"Why don't you take Joe along, or someone else, and leave Chris here? I'd feel a lot better with him here while you're gone."

She listens closely, and can tell by his breathing that he is out cold. Disturbed by her own thoughts, and thankful that John hasn't heard her, Vera closes her book, turns off the lamp, and gladly slips away from her dismal reality.

But tonight, she will be tormented by two vivid, powerful dreams.

In the first, she steps out of her back door into a clear summer's day. One with the bluest sky, and a perfect breeze that blows in from over the green fields. She sees Chris, leaning back against his truck with his arms folded, looking at the ground. She walks joyfully over to him, and notices that his expression is contorted with extreme sorrow, and tears run down his face. The dream ends when she hugs him, and begins to comfort him.

The second dream opens with the arrival of the blackest daytime sky she has ever seen. From the kitchen window, she sees ink colored clouds gather in a gray sky, and she hears the wind swirl with the power and force of warning. She is suddenly concerned over her husband's whereabouts, until she thinks she sees him hurrying down the gravel road towards the house. When she opens the door to call to him, she sees that it is Chris. Walking alone.

In the dark clouds behind him, Vera sees the sky's built up energy released—through a thick, jagged river of lightning—that stretches from the top of the sky all the way to the bottom. What follows is a clap of hideously loud treble thunder. The voice of cataclysm, sounding from one end of the Earth to the other. Immediately, she runs out to him and takes him by the hand, pulling him along until they are inside the house.

Where's John? she asks.

I didn't see him. I...

What is it, honey?

I'm scared, Vera, he says, and I don't know what to do...

At that moment, the thunder sounds again, loud enough to wake the dead—

Vera wakes up in the middle of the night, heart pounding so fast that she puts her hand to her chest and takes deep breaths. John lays beside her as usual. Resting comfortably in a deep sleep.

There are two things she knows she'll never forget. One is the Hellish storm. With clouds so dark, lightning so bright, and thunder so loud it can only exist in a dream. A dark symbol of approaching evil? Maybe.

The second thing is the young man himself. Around him, she had sensed a powerful longing. An *extreme* desire for purity and love, but mixed with a profound sorrow, and dread of the future.

While the Lady cries, she remembers the evil storm.

And her Angel.

19

I learned about abuse from my mother. Such are the goings on behind closed doors. I understand this while I go about my morning kitchen routine, my dress hiding the white cloth tied over what the knife had done. I come to know it, while I rub my aching wrist and the bruises on my side. Pain must be endured, I believe. It is the life I have been given. And the one I have chosen to live.

A splash of cold water to my face takes my breath. I gasp for air, as the water drips down onto my dress.

He stands up and steps close in front of me. Only hunger keeps him from spitting his eggs right into my face.

Did you *sass* me?

My whole leg suddenly throbs. I look at him bravely. But then he steps forward, pressing his boots onto both of my feet. I draw a sharp breath, pleading softly. He pushes both thumbs into my ribs.

Mother taught me to let the pain out through my voice. So, I do.

Shut up, he hisses. He holds me there. Without mercy. I lean against him and relax, enduring the pain, quietly howling away. A soft, *whoo-ing* sound. The pain jabs into my ribs and my poor feet, severe enough to make me think of being attacked in a dream by a demonic spirit. This is why I always wear shoes when he is at home.

Sometimes, I wonder why there can be no end to suffering.

Finally, he takes his boots off my gray slippers, and takes his thumbs off my ribs. I am so grateful that I hug him like he has given me a present. Pain absorbs the will. Robbing a person of their dignity.

We aren't going to pretend anymore. Between us is only the need to cause pain, the need for love, and the fear of loneliness and death.

We understand this now.

I think I *will* bring dinner, he says. And since you're in so much pain and can't cook, then maybe you're in too much pain to leave that bedroom anymore.

I just look at him. And pray to God he doesn't mean what I think.

I don't know why I don't just lock you in the closet, he says. Maybe its because I don't want you pissing all over my clothes.

I look deep into those blue eyes of his.

It is quiet. But it is there.

Life as you know it, he says, is over.

A strange look comes over his face. As though he has a quick flash of pain.

Or pity.

I'm gonna do what I should have done a long time ago. And if I find out you've left that bedroom. If I *ever* find out…

I turn away, hurrying quietly through the living room.

To my winter's prison.

He finishes breakfast in a haze of disbelief. Has it really come to this? When he is done, he goes in the bedroom to get his coat. I'm laying down, but I sit up painfully when he walks in. I watch him put on his jacket and gather up his keys, wallet and the black pocket knife.

I feel wispy. Like in a dream. Chris too, seems a lifeless version of himself. With no heart or soul, and very little tolerance for my pathetic condition.

But I will endure it. As I am accustomed to.

What I said, I meant, he admonishes, buttoning his denim coat. You are *never* to leave this room. I might park the truck down the road, and walk back and hide, so I can look through the window to see if you're still in here.

I stare. As dejectedly as ever.

Remember, he says.

Yes, sir.

Don't you call me that, he says sharply. I'm not your daddy.

I'm sorry.

You're always sorry. You make me sick to my stomach.

The comment hurts my feelings.

"I can't go outside anymore?"

You can't go outside this *room* anymore.

"What about the chickens?"

Don't you worry about those stupid chickens.

"Can I still go to the kitchen to get something to eat?" My voice has started to break already.

What did I just say, Elizabeth? I know you heard what I said.

"I know, but—"

I can't get used to the idea. I can't process it. I glance around the dreary little room, like I've never really seen it for what it is. It has never seemed quite so small. So dingy.

Chris steps slowly to where I am sitting, and kneels down on one knee. He puts his hands on the bed, on either side of me.

If you take one, single step past that bedroom door, he says, I'm going to take you outside, and tie you to that tree. And then I'm going to *nail* your right hand to the trunk.

I listen, and start to cry. Part of me believes he might actually do it.

How did you get that scrape on your hand? he says.

"It... it must have happened last night."

It was already there last night.

"Oh, *this* scrape. I... I fell outside."

How?

"I was going to the clothesline, and I f...fell when I was going down the s-steps."

He stares into me, checking me for a lie. But as clumsy as I am, I could very well be telling the truth. He'll never learn about my little trip down the long dirt road. Or about the letter I wrote and threw away.

You won't have to worry about the back steps anymore, will you?

I shake my head. The tears fall, but I do not wipe my eyes. The knife wound is burning into me like it just happened. I imagine a big spot of blood is on the bed, underneath my leg.

I'm goin' to work now, he says. Now what did I say about you leaving this room?

"I can't leave it…"

He watches me descend. I plead with dark eyes, which lately, seem always red and full of tears.

There is no pleasure in it for him. But he understands now, that he couldn't have stopped it if he tried.

So he surrendered to it.

20

The sound of hammering awakens me. I raise my head and see my husband outside the window, driving several nails into the wood. I'm disoriented... *What time is it?* I focus on the clock radio, and see that it's just after 12:30. Chris had made the rare lunchtime trip to the house. To take care of some unfinished business.

But the foundations of my prison had been laid a long time ago, and fear had already built an impenetrable barrier.

I hadn't planned on going anywhere...

Except to the bathroom, to get rid of the water I poured into myself right after he had left. I had gone straight to the bathroom sink, and drank so much water that I stretched my stomach. The radio had been no comfort, and I was in no mood for writing in my notebook. So I had rested, and let sleep have its way.

The hammering is driving into my skull. Sharpening my nerves to a razor's edge. I get up from the bed and hobble into the bathroom. The sleep has actually helped a little. My headache is gone, and my wounds don't hurt as badly. But every muscle from my neck down was sore, and I feel very stiff and weak. The noise goes on, until over two dozen large nails have been driven into the wood. From the bathroom, I hear the hammer slam loudly into the back of the truck. The engine starts, and the truck drives away.

When I am done, I look at myself in the mirror. I see a pale face, with long, black hair, framing eyes that are indefinably sad. It looks like I haven't slept in days. I want to take a bath. But the cut aches so badly…

I start to run the water in the tub, until I remember my poor chickens—

It flashes at me again. Like a light.

I have to shake the thought from my head. Already, my heart rate quickens. But I turn the water back on, and run a bathtub of warm water.

The cut is in the back of my left thigh, and is no more than an inch long. But it is deep, and very painful. It feels like a single rod of throbbing pain, burning red heat into the rest of my leg. It hurts for me to walk on it, and it causes me to limp like I have a twisted ankle. While I undress, I remember about the pain capsules. There are only a handful of them left. I remember them, as I slip into the bathtub. The water is cooler than I thought it would be. It is soothing to the wound. I am very glad for this diversion, and I close my eyes, sliding further into the water.

Pills.

A few months back, when the bottle was full, I had thought about them. A lot.

Sometimes I have to wonder. Why did the only two people I ever loved seem to despise me so much? I can picture the look on his face, the look in his eyes during it all. It's as though he's doing it to someone else, like he forgets that its me he's burning or cutting. He seems possessed, like he's out of his mind. Yet, there's a frightening lucidity. A terrifying awareness of what he's doing. There's an overwhelming coldness that envelopes him, a spirit of merciless evil. Truthfully, it's a miracle that I'm still alive. Perhaps, he *does* love me. I feel like the two of us are in a vortex. Swirling and spinning towards a center of evil.

I feel abandoned by God himself. Only a blind exercising of pure Faith seems to keep me in touch with Him. But there's a dark presence that I sense around me. And it's always there. It seems responsible for it all, including the strange coldness in the house, and the shadows in the corners. It put the nails in the window today, and made the jagged hole appear in the bathroom door a long time ago. I turn my head, and look at the old cloth tacked over that hole.

The bathroom suddenly feels like a tomb.

So I lay my head back, and rest in my watery grave.

The sun disappears behind the clouds, and my world is covered in gray. The cold air has found it way south, resting heavy on the eastern county. Winter is arriving early this year. With each passing hour, I wish more and more that there was a fireplace in the bedroom. The radio is alive with talk of Christmas. Handel is strong on my mind this year.

The two of us don't bother with Christmas anymore. Not since that Christmas night when I smelled that burning plastic-rubbery odor, after the artificial tree was tossed in the fireplace. I remember that the burned metal branch holders looked like long, skeletal finger claws, when I pulled them out of the ashes the next day.

My classical station has betrayed me. Today of all days. There is only static where it usually is. I've been checking it every few minutes for the last three hours. Finally, I admit defeat, and leave it to the contemporary Christian station.

Four o'clock...

I should be preparing to cook. Or taking clothes off the line, or gazing at the barren field and trees. Humming or whistling loudly, as I go about the end of the day's business. Enduring the banality, and hoping for the three thousandth time that this day after sunset was going to be different. Today, I hope he is going to shove the broom into my hand, and make me sweep the living room and the kitchen. Then, he'll make me cook his pork chops and fried potatoes. I'll limp around like an arthritic old woman, playing it up for all its worth, reminding him that a good stabbing is probably enough, at least until after the Christmas season.

Southern fried pork chops. And fried potatoes with onions…

With peach pie for dessert…

My nerves tingle just a little—maybe with genuine apprehension.

I'm hungry.

This morning I was too tired, and my body was in too much pain. I thought I wouldn't be able to walk or eat for days. But the nap and the bath did more good than I expected. I'm getting restless, and I want something to eat.

Parts of me are fleshy enough. There are a few pounds for me to give safely. Especially from my breasts. *"Those big betties"* Mother had called them. One of the all time examples of the pot calling the kettle black.

Hunger…

It always happens, when the mind tells the body that the food supply might be cut off. What would he do if I cleaned the floor up, and surprised him with dinner? What did he say he would do?

The tree…

Which is why the hunger is slowly forgotten. I limp back to the bathroom, and take three more of the generic pills. The bathroom is as clean as it needs to be. And so is the bedroom. But I'm too nervous to relax, and there are no melodies to write.

What I really want is to get out of this dingy little room, even if its only for a minute. I open the bedroom door, and stare twisted reality right into its eyes.

A single step…

I close the door, and wander over to the window. Every inch of the sky I can see is cloudy. It reminds me of snow weather. I sit down on the foot of the bed, staring at the outside world. The window frames for me a view of the leafless tree skeletons, which twist and scratch their way upward, into a sky of premature cold and darkness.

> *A spring tree in waiting*
> *Is my heart indeed*
> *A soul's winter pain*
> *Has laid claim in misery*
>
> *The waiting tree*
> *Has no solace from days of living*
> *No rest from a weary path chosen*
> *No sleep for a burdened spirit*
>
> *A spring tree in waiting*
> *Has no leaves of Summer's Tears*
> *Spring's hour hath no power to shine—*
> *Upon this day of fear*

The Earth is two weeks away from its darkest hour.
The Solstice.
It's only five o'clock…
But it's getting dark.

I wouldn't have been outside today anyway. The clouds have swallowed the sunset, and the air is chilly. But for the first time in weeks, dinner won't be ready when he gets home.

I have obeyed. Not one step outside the room.

My hair is out, and brushed long. My black, shiny hair spills about my shoulders, and down the length of my back. When my hair is down, I am imposing to the house shadows. I fix myself up the best I can in a plain navy dress. I make use of my only pair of sheer stockings, which I never wear, so they still look new. My one good pair of black shoes are an inch high. I check the bathroom mirror again, and am prompted to undo the top button on my dress.

A country Carmen.

Painfully, I ease down on the edge of the bed, grimacing against the throbbing in my leg. I put my legs together, imagining that he'll open the bedroom door, and be dazzled by demure, voluptuous power. I do my best hair toss, with natural flair in private, and glare at the door with a smoldering expression.

My loving, forgiving husband will burst through the door in tears of sorrow and sweep me into his arms, kissing me passionately from head to toe until I shudder—

He's home

The truck reminds me of how ugly and stupid I usually feel. I put my top button back into place, and almost consider putting up my hair. I open the bedroom door, and wait for my loving husband to walk in the house.

Chris opens the front door, and steps wearily inside. He is carrying two brown bags of takeout food. The bags have those little grease spots on them, that warns of something deliciously fattening inside. His cold, exhausted expression slaps me with reality.

"Hey, sweetie,"

It came out more timidly than I had wanted it to. I am suddenly very nervous, and hide my body behind the door, watching him clump through the living room as if I'm not even here. His keys clink onto the kitchen table, followed by the bags of food. I listen hungrily as he opens a soda, and plops a fork noisily into a plate.

I hadn't been sure what it was, until now. I can smell it.

Oh, no

Griffin's Barbecue. A Martin County take out. A matchbox of a restaurant, whose chopped barbecue could be sold nationally. But the owner has no such ambition. He is quietly making a fortune.

I close my eyes and breathe it in, trying to taste the air. But its not happening. I haven't eaten since yesterday and this is one of my favorite meals. I stand at the door, biting my fingernail, and staring at the old wooden floor in front of me.

Should I ask him?

I imagine my voice triggering something inside him, activating something evil in his brain.

But I am so hungry.

Chris.. can I...

I imagine him running into the room, jabbing the fork into my lower back and punching me hard on the thigh, over the knife wound. My breathing quickens. Wisely, I decide against bothering him while he eats. I close the door again, hobbling over to the chair. After turning on the radio, I pick up my Rose Diaries, and lose myself in a poetic scribbling or two.

The hours move along, until my world is under cover of night. We had gone to bed without incident. Earlier when he took off his belt, I started to shake. But he only tossed it in the closet and went to take his bath. Now, I'm lying in the dark beside him. Wide awake and starving.

"Christopher, can I have something to eat?"

My voice startles him from the edge of sleep, which he had *really* been looking forward to tonight.

"Chris, honey? Can I go and just taste something to eat? I just want a small taste, please? Chris, please?"

He has to stop himself from elbowing me in the ribs.

"I just want one spoonful. Just one."

A plateful

"I didn't eat breakfast, remember? Remember, Chris? Can I please…"

In the next instant, I feel myself being lifted up from the bed. My journey continues, and there is a curious sensation of flight, until I land in a clumsy heap on the cold, dark floor.

A startling noise. It sounds like two people have fallen together and broken their clumsy necks.

The fall re-ignites the fire in my leg. Self-loathing curses my stupidity, while I pull my old winter coat from the dark closet. I swallow three more of the pain capsules, limp over to the chair, and settle into my uncomfortable place for the night.

The dying glow from the fireplace is barely visible. The light is too weak to reveal the shadows, which taunt me from every cold, black corner of the room.

A chimney

The coat blanket smells of ashe and silhouette, as I close my eyes, and try as hard as I can to fall asleep.

21

The subconscious.

What a marvelous thing!

The Piano Concerto No. 23 in A. Mozart's subtle expression of beauty and indefinable sadness. A single breath of emotion from beginning to end. I had heard this concerto only once on the radio, many years before I was married. I liked it well enough, but was not overwhelmed by its quiet, understated charm. In the cold, dark confines of my winter's prison, my mind expands while I sleep, until a new imagination envelops me—one so complete and vivid that it becomes my world, indistinguishable from my waking reality.

"Ladies and gentlemen, it is my honor, and great privilege to introduce to you our soloist for this evening, a woman who needs no introduction the world over, Miss Carmen Angelina Coletti."

I glide onto the stage in confidence and humility, draped in full length white. My black hair flows freely about my shoulders and back, giving startling contrast to the silvery white, silken evening gown. I stand in awe of both the Opera house, and my own lack of fear before the enthusiastic crowd. Every seat is filled with men and women of all ages and nationalities. There are three levels of balconies above the main floor, all done in beautiful red with golden trim, glowing softly under subdued lighting. The balconies flow around me in a massive semicircle of hidden cheers, and thunderous applause.

Carmen Coletti's piano playing is known the world over. Coletti. Equally renowned for her ability to mimic nineteenth century *bel canto* style. A style that emphasizes melodic brilliance and virtuosity. Italian Overtures, after the manner of Rossini, are her stock and trade. Coletti overtures are famous for their ability to confound experts with exactness of form. And *extreme* melodic inspiration. Many have dismissed her as a fraud, believing her to be manufactured by a group of gifted composers. Hoaxed onto the world through this virtuoso.

She's as despised, as she is loved.

But these enemies are harmless.

I pull myself away from the warmth and beauty of my view and reception, then sit down to the grand piano at center stage.

The conductor raises his baton of magic—

And from the huge orchestra pit comes the shadowy opening chords, which travel to the far corners of the large opera house, and echo perfectly, bathing every listener in depth of breathtaking sound. I know already, that the performance will be perfect... and that when its over I am going to *eat*. A lot.

When the introduction ends, *I strike the first note without fear, to send the word of the Lord to them. The smooth, velvet tone of this piano is the Grieving Land of my youth, to exceed the beauty of all made by human hands. I can only smile when I look forward in the bars, to see the notes of this Nativity born from such an instrument. From the sound of the winds, the colors I see, I know this performance to be Divinely Inspired, to be a part of the infinity, the landscape which is my fervent memory.* I play every part, listening, *feeling* every note and chord. The accompaniment is full. Richly textured. Uniquely inspired.

On the trail to Golgotha. Upon the keys of this adagio, I am at a loss for rational thought, as the tears come to my eyes immediately. I am transported back to the world of ashen gray regret, to the farm where she lives in the deepest sorrow, waiting to be lifted up, and drawn so near unto Him. But I see her longing coalesce into a driving rainfall, to crush and drown her spirit to death. I see the colors of my youth on the farm, born from more grief than I can endure, even while these winds attempt to laugh through the river of tears they cry. As I play the rest of this adagio for my Savior at the Cross, I am carried along the timeline, to where I stroll the fields of my salvation, searching for where it is that my beloved mother could have gone. In the haunting winds, I even hear the chiming of the whistle train, which sings a refrain, that of pain itself, and the sorrow conceived and born in my time. Soon, my last note fades into the orchestra, which answers in a Divine whisper of wind.

In the driving rain, I brave the wind on this Road of Hope—to the tomb of my Lord and Savior. I walk this road when my mother has gone, grieving our time at the foot of the Cross, and his burial in the Tomb. In the storm of rising wind, I push forward through the gray, down the long dirt road, to stand at the door of the tomb; to receive his blessing once again. But what is this! In the torrent of water and wind, I stand at the door of an empty tomb—seeing the great stone rolled away! As I turn to leave—the Melody of Hope dances freely in the clouds, as I remember the report of what some have said, that He is risen. I breeze joyfully through the finale, able to see the keys more clearly as my fingers move, as they *flow* the closing scales of this *Passion* in A. The final notes are played, and the Players of Orchestra's Light breathe the perfect ending to their night of perfect harmony.

I stand up quickly from the piano, out of courtesy to the roaring crowd, which pours upon me the grandest appreciation imaginable. I wipe my eyes, holding back the rest of the tears, pleasantly ignoring screams for an encore. I notice the beautiful chandelier, resting proudly above the madness, and I glance once more at the crimson balconies. As humbly as I can, I motion to my orchestra and conductor, nestled in the soft lighting of the pit, just below the stage. My players take a bow themselves to screams of appreciation and bold, vulgar yells to hear one of my overtures.

I'm so hungry

The Opera house begins to melt away. The applause is slowly, smoothly replaced by the light pattering of cold rain on the rusty tin roof.

I am curled in the chair, crying in the dark. But not from sadness.

I am happy.

There you go. Good dog.

Eat it all up, like the greedy sow pig that you are.

I ignore my mind's cruelty (a woman's voice), as I shove the sweet cole slaw into my mouth by the spoonful.

There had only been a taste of barbecue left. Chris had fixed himself a sandwich for breakfast, and took one with him for lunch. I'm lucky that I got to taste it at all. The taste had rung through my mouth and into my ears like an alarm, then sent a wave of satisfaction into the rest of my body. Now, I ravage the sweet coleslaw, which is hardly less satisfying.

At the least, I'm finally eating. It is my first meal in two days. He had shown mercy, and thrown the bag and a plastic spoon into the room on the floor. I had bent nervously over like a zoo monkey and picked it up.

Thank you so much, Honey, I had said.

The words had hardly left my mouth, when the bedroom door was closed and locked, and he was driving to his daily escape from the shadow house. He goes to work all the time, even when the other farmhands stay home. It's cold and rainy today, and he could have taken the day off. But Chris went in anyway. There is always something to do. Something to fix or clean. Or someone he might get lucky enough to see. Anything to get away from this house, and the pathetic thing in the bedroom. It is now shoving coleslaw and cornbread into its red lipped mouth, devouring in big, greedy bites.

I finish every bit of the pound of slaw, and all five sticks of the cold, grainy cornbread. I don't remember the last time I enjoyed a meal so much.

My daily routine, such as it is, has been destroyed. There are now no chickens to feed. No rooms to sweep. No dishes to wash. No meals to thaw and cook, and no clothes to hang outside.

And no sunset.

I can hear the noisy hens. Are they hungry? How they would love swallowing crumbled bits of the cornbread! I wonder if they can taste the difference between corn grain and corn bread.

It won't be like this forever…

Things will get better soon.

I suddenly feel very sad, because I know I can never run away.

Some would accuse me of being a little slow. A little cuckoo. But maybe there is a Divine purpose. A stubborn, irrepressible Faith and devotion to the Will of God. What happens, simply happens, and there is nothing I can do about it. Nothing I have the right to do. There is a solemn calling to perform, and all things work together for good—to them who love God.

Isolation and confinement come very natural to some. I am a recluse from the Old School—no people, no problem. And I have been trained by the best. Barbara Coletti taught me the meaning of isolation.

So, the first thing I will do, is to forget about the outside. I will put the tree, the chickens, and the sunset out of my mind. I will relax, and allow the bathroom, the closet and the bedroom to become my world. I thank God for the small view through the bedroom window, and for the radio, with its music and voices for company…

But most of all, I am thankful for this schizophrenic, *synesthesian* world of melody I have access to. A crazy, strange place where sounds have substance, shape, and color. It begins to occupy my mind, as my eyes twitch back and forth. I watch and listen to the structures form before my eyes. A miracle of genetics, passed down through my father's blood, from my grandfather. Michelangelo Coletti, who was seriously accused of sorcery by at least one of his ignorant acquaintances. His fellow migrants, and even his wife Alicia, my *good* grandmother, had cowered in a ridiculous fearfulness over his skill with the guitar and the fiddle. He was only 36 when he died, when my father, Michael, was just a boy. Through the Coletti bloodline it flows, resting upon this poor self, who lacks the ambition or bravery to show it to another living soul. The means by which me and my husband might have found a different life. A better life.

I sit in the cold room, propped up in the bed under the covers, lost in that strange world where violins talk with voices of color, and all the instruments play sounds according to their own will. I watch as strings and winds begin to conspire—building an orchestral frame of simple complexities and inspired simplicity.

And now, the orchestral is joined by my classical piano. I watch, and then close my eyes to listen.

An extreme level of melodic purity. A *Winter Concerto*, for piano and orchestra.

For my notebook.

22

*T*his is the biggest year we've ever had, John says. I should retire.

"If you knew *what*," Vera says, "you'd hire a foreman."

"Why do I need to pay somebody to do my work?" John is sitting at their big kitchen table, wearing glasses that make him look too scholarly, squinting at papers spread out all over the place. "How 'bout I put you out there. That'll straighten 'em out, won't it?"

Vera ignores him, and tends to her dinner on the stove. Pig's knuckles. And cabbage. Something she cooks for variety's sake only, when she is just plain sick of everything else under the sun and in the refrigerator. The whole mess had been boiled tender, and is now sizzling together in a frying pan, searing, seasoning to perfection.

Pigs knuckles.

I should go see the doctor. I think I'm getting sick...

I can't stop thinking about dying.

"Chris left early today, didn't he?"

"Yeah," John sighs. "Your *boyfriend* left early."

The comment reaches up and slaps her hard.

"What's that supposed to mean?"

"Must've hit a nerve," he says.

"Why would you say something like that?" she asks, trying to sound offended.

"I'm just teasin', honey."

"I don't think I'm partial to *that* kind of teasing. You must have had a reason for saying something so..."

True.

"Maybe," he says.

"Maybe what?"

"Maybe I did have a reason."

She waits for him to continue. Fearfully.

"There's somethin' you gotta admit," he says. "You been takin' a lotta walks lately. It's about the only time you ever come outta that room."

"Since when is it a crime for a woman to take a walk on her own property?"

"Since when have you been so interested in unloadin' and stackin' grain?"

"So you don't want me around anymore?"

"Vera they've all noticed it."

"Noticed *what*?"

He takes his glasses off, and rubs his eyes.

"A blind man could see it," he says.

"John, I want you to stop this foolishness, and tell me what you're talking about."

"I'm talkin' about the fact that you've been hangin' around up there more this year than you have the last *ten* years."

"I thought you were glad to see me all those times," she says, a little hurt.

"Well, I might have been, if I'd thought you were there to see *me.*"

Their last thought hangs in the air. Taunting. Daring them to say another word.

"Well, I… I have been missin' you a lot lately…"

"Aw, come off it, Vera, you haven't missed me that much in fifteen years."

"So you don't want me to come up there anymore? Do I embarrass you? You don't want the men lookin' at your bored, big tittied wife bouncin' around?"

"It's nothin' like that and you know it."

"Well then what is it? First, you're screamin' at me to get out of the house more, and now this. No one notices me when I go up there anyway."

A dreadful pause.

"What is it b'tween you and him?"

"Me and *who*?"

" Don't do that," he says.

"Huh?"

"Don't stand there and act like I just got in off a mule wagon, Vera. You've gotta be kiddin' me."

John stands up from the table, clumping boots slowly to where she stood. She stiffens, preparing for whatever he is going to say. Or do.

"How blind do you think I am?"

"I don't know what you're talking—"

" I said, don't *do* that!" His tone is loud, and rather vicious. His teeth are grimaced. "You think I haven't seen the way you two act? You can't get within ten feet of each other without gigglin' and fidgetin' like a couple of school kids, Vera. I've seen it with my own eyes. They've all seen it."

"Well stop beatin' around it then," she hisses.

He almost said it. But what if he is wrong? The man probably just has that affect on women...

"I'm not accusing you of anything," he says. "I'm just tellin' you what I've seen, Vera. The way it looks..."

"What are you accusing me of?"

Her voice is low. Whispery. A winter's worth of tension is forming.

"We'll talk when you're feelin' a bit more honest about it," he says.

"Honest ab...John, where are you going?"

He gathers his keys and denim coat, and goes fuming out of the house towards the big, forest green F-something pickup. His country refuge.

The Lady empties the frying pan over the trash, until her dinner is thrown away.

Her husband had just walked out the door—

But Vera's heart is aching for another.

Another.

23

Christmas Eve.

Its been *two weeks* since the gate was laid, and the barbecue breakfast was eaten. Already, ten pounds are gone. The waif can be seen waiting inside my figure. But the curves remain, though not quite as remarkable, nor as difficult to fathom.

Chris only comes into the room to sleep. And to bathe. At night, when he is on the bed, I have to take my place on the floor. He won't let me sleep in the chair. I use two sheets over some dresses for a mattress, with an old blanket, and my winter coat for linen. But at least he hasn't touched me. And the knife wound doesn't hurt anymore.

117

My concerto had come to me complete during a single hour, and in three days I had worked it out, scribbling it down the best I know how. Probably a masterpiece in light classical form. It came to me in the key of A major.

Who knows why that particular key.

Conceived in a lively vein, with great melodic purity, simple texture, and rhythmic freedom reminiscent of Italian comic opera. Doomed by Fate, to probably go unperformed for the rest of time and history.

But this cold, Christmas Eve brings no original music to Signora Elisabetta. Only chills. And hunger.

Thankfully, the fireplace is blazing, and the bedroom door is open. He is always home now, always in the living room or the kitchen, or outside working on or sitting in that black truck, listening to his country station. He doesn't even want to look at me. And he doesn't want to be in the house with me either. But truthfully, he has nowhere else to go.

He had cooked bacon this morning. And he didn't offer me a single slice. Not one bite. But how was I supposed to say anything about it? He hasn't hurt me since the knife wound, and I don't want to risk it. But I can't take the hunger anymore. It is painful.

Maybe just one slice of bread. Or two slices, with jelly…

I've even started to hallucinate. Sometimes, I can swear there is a starving cat outside the window. The same white one that sits on the windowsill every other night in my dreams, clawing against the glass, desperate for a small meal.

I have to eat something…

I have to

Two days ago, he baked cinnamon rolls. They had done their job well, causing me to pound on the door, begging him through tears. My howling had sent evil sorrow through him in waves. But he had endured it as he was accustomed, frosted and ate one, then threw the rest to the blackbirds. This is my third day without food. And he had cooked himself a good Christmas Eve breakfast of bacon, scrambled eggs and buttered grits.

I steady myself, and gather my nerve. I focus on a spot just beyond the open door, and begin to put my right foot forward…

The truck cranks, and I yip like a whipped Brittany, yanking my foot back into the room. I listen as Fate has mercy on my poor hunger, sending my husband driving down the road, away on some quick errand or another. I relax and take my time, creeping through the field of hidden traps and danger.

To what bizarre end have I come to! What strange place is this, where I am imprisoned, sneaking across the floor of my house, hoping to steal scraps of food from my own kitchen!

I tiptoe as quietly as a hungry mouse. There on the stove, lying on a paper towel in a plate, is six pieces of brown sugar cured bacon, and a small pot of butter flavored grits.

His errand is over.

He comes into the dreary house, ignoring the misery covered walls. In the kitchen, he notices the left over food on the stove.

Fearfully, he goes to the tool shack. He picks up the hammer, but changes his mind.

The hatchet is better.

In dread, his footsteps are slow, and heavy in the cold house…

" I didn't mean it, Chris… Chris, you know I didn't mean to… help me not to do it… Please talk to me about it, and have mercy for me… Please, Christopher… I didn't mean to…"

I awaken with a start. Wondering why there is no light. My mind renders *What Child Is This,* hardly protecting my bones from the bitter, biting cold. When I move, my face brushes the clean, soapy smell of one of my dresses.

The closet…

I don't have to ask if I dreamed it all. The fire in my bound wrists, and the cold in my body tells me it is real. With my mind, I take a macabre inventory of every part of my body. The icy air is hard to breathe.

There is no light.

24

*T*he arctic wind moved over the mountains. Blowing swiftly above the forests and fields, until winter had settled in the eastern county. The rains came, and were quickly frozen as they fell from the clouds, covering the land in layers of ice and snow. I stand at the window, peering through the haze at the gray world outside. The tree skeletons are all coated with ice—icicles frozen in time—thwarted on their journey to the safety of the white ground below.

Its been two months since the gates fell closed on my winter's prison. Not a single time since have I stepped outside the locked bedroom door. When my music is silent, and when my husband is occupied or away, there are things my mind forces me to remember. As I look at the ice and snow, I am forced to remember my mother.

Many children endure severe, continuous punishment and abuse. For most, it is in the name of correction. Training and nurture. "Train a child in the way he should go," and such. The lectures about why the child is going to suffer are preached to them, as they sit trembling in terror of the rod of discipline.

Barbara Coletti made no speeches.

This happened when I was thirteen years old.

The snow had fallen the night before. The ground is covered in a beautiful field of white. I am at my bedroom window, staring with longing at the new snow. I already asked my mother once could I go outside.

I go into the living room where she is engaged in a book. She is lovely. And powerfully sensual. With a smooth, creamy complexion, piercing gray eyes and black hair to match her daughter's. I try not to notice what she does when I walk into the room.

She rolls her eyes in contempt.

" Momma?"

She doesn't answer. She doesn't even look up.

I sit down on the couch beside her, noticing how much warmer it is in the living room.

I am afraid of my mother. But I love her, and worship her. I lean boldly into her personal space and kiss her full, and lovingly on the mouth.

"You're beautiful."

"Why are you bothering me, Elizabeth?"

" Do you want me to sweep the snow off the front steps?"

She doesn't answer.

"I'll sweep the snow off the front steps if you want, Momma."

My voice is meek, with a touch of sadness. Already I am a fearful and somber child. But I have gathered my nerve, and am determined to convince her to let me out of my prison, so I can go play in the snow.

"You wouldn't mind if I put my coat on and went out for about five minutes, would you?"

Her gaze slowly lifts from the book, and she locks eyes with me.

It had all started when I was an infant. Barbara would lay on top of her baby, and listen to her scream.

She closes her book calmly, then puts it away. She begins to gently stroke her daughter's hair…

And then slowly, deliberately, she wraps part of Carmen's black, shiny hair around her beautiful hand…

And she begins to pull.

Slowly. Deliberately. Until my face is twisted in pain. She sits me calmly onto the couch and straddles me, pinning me against the back cushion.

" I just wanted to sweep the snow, Momma. I'm sorry."

Behind closed doors—

Nobody's business.

"You're not sorry," she says.

"Momma, please don't…"

"You are a stubborn, willful little *bitch*. And I won't have it."

She pulls my hair hard, listening to me howl gently from the pain. But she isn't satisfied...

With her other hand, she grabs my ear and twists it without mercy. I start to wail loudly, nearly screaming. Barbara watches her daughter's hope fade, and she watches the tears pour down my face. She pulls and twists once more with all her might, and I finally let out a piercing scream.

And then Barbara holds me there. And watches me.

"I told you not to ask me again, didn't I?"

"Yes, Momma."

"Now get up and go in my bedroom. She lets me up, follows me into the room and takes her leather belt from the closet. Without another word, she grabs my hair and begins to whip me as hard as she can. Every inch of me, she whips. I flail, begging and screaming, as mother brings the belt down over and over across my legs, arms and back.

She isn't correcting me. Or chastising me.

She is teaching me a lesson.

How dare I be bold enough to ask to play in the snow, when she told me not to ask again! How dare I look her in the eye without fear! Barbara Jean Coletti is determined, that she will someday achieve a level of dominance and control over her daughter that most mothers have never dared imagine.

I can see the belt lashes flying. The walls seem to stretch upward forever. And mother's beautiful face is cold and stern, with a near frown from the effort. Her grip is strong, and the powerful blows send sharp, stinging pains into my skin. Loud and clear is the sound of the belt cutting into me, and the sound of my own pathetic, hopeless screaming.

Mother beats me until she runs out of strength. Until my screams grow hoarse.

But like all the others, it ended.

"Get up from there, and look at me." She is nearly winded. "So, you want to go play in the snow?"

"No, Momma. I'll go to my room and I'll be quiet."

"Put my belt away. And go put on your coat."

Bewildered, I quickly do as Mother asks. She takes me by the arm, pulls me out the back door, then flings me hard into the snow. I can only watch as she marches back into the house and slams the door. Locking it behind me

This is what I remember, as I stand at the window of my bedroom, looking out at the ice and snow. Mother had left me outside that cold February day, until well after dark.

I remember the cold.

And the twilight.

The way the tree skeletons seemed to grow, slowly twisting into otherworldly shapes of foreboding. I remember the nightfall, and how there were no stars to comfort me. Only a dark gray sky which soon turned black, and pressed down on me.

I had loved my Mother. And I sometimes cried, because my mother had despised me. Even now as an adult I lower my head. And feel the tears drip onto my dress.

I wish I'd never been born.

Momma, I didn't want you to leave. Where did you go? Why didn't you come back?

It's always so cold. I'm so cold and afraid every day.

Why did you have to go?

Why did you hurt me?

You were supposed to protect me. But you were always hurting me. Always whipping and beating me, threatening to do terrible things, making me feel ugly and stupid. And maybe I was, but were you supposed to make me feel that way?

You were never kind to me.

You never told me that you loved me.

I turn my gaze from the icy world outside the window. I look at my portrait of the little flower girl. I stare into her sad eyes, wondering what kind of life she had. If she had been mistreated. If her mother had loved her.

Maria.

He had taken the smallest amount of pity, and used it to buy a heater. My chair and radio stand are pulled away from the cold window, and are tucked in the corner by the closet. It allows me to sit comfortably and read my Bible, listen to the radio, or write my music and still see the window. The little heater is barely adequate, but it keeps me just warm enough so I don't have to wear a coat all the time. But at night its different. The cold nights on the floor are so brutal, that sometimes it feels like the heater isn't even plugged in.

My last night in the chair resulted in a sore wrist, when he woke up in the middle of the night to go to the bathroom. He had yanked me out of the chair by my hair, and thrown me to the other side of the room.

I will never sleep in the chair again.

What if I get pregnant again?

If we had children, things would be different. He wouldn't treat them the way he treats me.

But I wonder…

It might be a selfish thing for me to bring a child into this horrible place. To be born is to be cursed, and to live is to suffer.

I wish I wasn't afraid of people. Sometimes I want to go out into the world, and just help people feel better about themselves. To help ease pain and suffering.

Wherever Momma is, I hope she's safe.

I hope she's happy.

I suddenly feel the hunger pains in my body.

But I endure it, as I am accustomed to.

I think I'm going crazy.

Sometimes when I'm in the dark, I feel like something will reach out to me, and take me by the throat, and just look into my eyes until I faint from fear.

A shadow.

Would I survive, if Chris left me here? Will I survive if he stays?

If a man ever gets his hands on you, she always said. And then she would shake her head and laugh at me. So many things she said about me came true. So many things. I'm her prophecy, made flesh.

But sometimes she was glad I was around. Every now and then she didn't yell at me or threaten me, or call me names.

Lizbeth, she would say.

She was beautiful. And so powerful. So strong.

I still love her.

I close my eyes, feeling the music flow from pain, through my imagination and into my memory…

A small, melancholy piece of epic simplicity. Played from the piano in my mind's cathedral.

For my mother.

25

I wake up on the cold floor. Howling to the top of my lungs. After a few seconds I realize where I am, and I'm able to stop screaming. The glow from my little heater is kept confined by the pitch blackness, and its warmth is captured and dispersed by the cold.

Everyone thinks they are prepared to die. The depressed even dream of it fondly. People of faith see it as a gate to Paradise. Heathens see it as an eternal rest. A glorious sleep.

But Death is a fearsome creature.

It extends long, icy hands into my heart almost every day and night, moving images through my body and into my mind. Nightmares of being chased are standard for me. They always have been. But my dreams have become simpler. Larger and less reflective of my reality. Fears and pathologies…

Nightmares of cold, dark forests. Nighttime deserts, deep caves and caverns. Mysterious swamps, endless oceans… always alone, with no hope of survival. Tonight, my mind had taken me on an icy trip with my husband. I find myself a passenger of fear, being driven to the middle of a frozen wasteland of white and pure crystalline cold. There is only a field of ice and snow, stretching into every corner of the earth. An endless expanse. A lonely death.

He throws me out of the black truck and speeds away. Far away. I am left totally alone, and I know I am going to die. The cold seems to take my breath, while the blue sky immediately begins to darken…

Mercifully, I wake up before the nightfall of my dream. Screaming. And when I realize where I am, I immediately shut my mouth and pray I didn't wake him up.

Some say that stress can cause nightmares. That a stressful day can lead to a night plagued with fearful images. Had my twilight been a stressful one?

After sunset, he had come into the room without words, and pulled me from a good daydream. He had snatched me out of my chair and shoved a rag into my mouth, using another one to gag me by tying it around. He flipped me monstrously onto the bed and sat on my back, exposing my legs and backside. With the piece of wood he had brought with him, he proceeded to bruise, and split the skin on my buttocks and the backs of my thighs, until I was too tired to kick. And then he continued, listening to me cry with the cloth stuffed in my mouth, until my backside and thighs were purple and bloody from top to bottom.

It had taken a long time to achieve. Everytime he would sit still, I'd thought it was over. And then he would go to work on another part of my leg, until the skin was opened up, and the blood was present. Not trickling or running. Just present. It left my buttocks and legs black and purple, with huge, hard patches of skin that felt like something rough and hard had been implanted underneath. And the bloody welts were extremely severe, and as numerous as they had ever been.

Was my twilight a stressful one? Had I suffered enough stress to have had a nightmare about abandonment and death?

I wonder if I will live to see another Christmas, as I lay on the bed the next morning. My radio is on. The classical station seems to have mercy, playing one good selection after another. It feels good lying on the bed. The bed is soft and warm. Sometimes I'll drift and have peaceful, restful naps.

I suddenly cough. Violently enough to make my throat sore. The cold nights on the floor sometimes fills my lungs, and I'll spend half the next day coughing it up. I seem to cough a lot more these days.

I have the sniffles so badly it feels like I have a cold. And I can still taste that soapy rag that was in my mouth. I brushed my teeth three times to try to get rid of the taste. My buttocks and the backs of my legs are so sore that I can barely walk. It feels like arthritis. And the burning, itchy tingling is bad enough to make me touch them, and often I am amazed at how the skin feels.

Broken.

Damaged—

And broken.

What a person doesn't know, can't hurt them.

If a person is born into misery, they don't know what a better life is like. They simply cope with the one they have, and the hardships it offers. And they learn to endure. Like when a bird's cage is opened, and it just sits there. The poor creature doesn't know about escape and freedom, so it doesn't hurt when the cage is closed again. My body is so battered that I can barely walk. But what else is there? I'm not crying, and sobbing for my poor body. I've never had a life without pain. So it doesn't hurt, when I think about the way he had beaten me until I could only grunt and tremble in agony.

I just lay here. Coughing. Resting. Listening to music. Not knowing that after tonight, hope will vanish away forever.

But sometimes, even for the accursed, the natural light will glimmer. And I will pray to be rescued from the evening day.

And I will wonder why there can be no end to suffering.

26

Days come and go

As do the Seasons

Until the Earth has made another journey—

And it is Winter again

Vera! Vera are you alright in there?

"I was until you woke me up. What do you want?"

I want you to stop this foolishness, John says, and get out of that bedroom. You've been locked up in there off and on for the whole damned year, and I'm *sick* of it!

"Don't you have anything better to do?"

John slams on the door again. Pointlessly.

"John, why don't you leave me alone?"

Vera, get up, and open this door or else.

"Or else *what*?" she laughs. "What are you gonna do, kick the door down and beat me up? Big strong man?"

John hears her laughing to herself, from behind the door of her Gray Palace.

Vera, honey, how do you expect to get any better if you never come out of that room?

"I'll be alright," she says, coughing. "I just need some rest."

That's what you said *last* Christmas, when you first started lockin' yourself in here for weeks at a time. Now when is enough gonna be enough? You only come out to eat and then its right back in that room.

"So I'm a fattenin' hog, now, is that it?"

You're slimmin' up enough to make me worry about you, Viv.

"So I've lost a few pounds," she says. "Big deal. My jeans were too tight anyway."

Well, what are you gonna do about Christmas?

"Christmas?"

Are we going to Conrad and Brenda's?

Oh, God...

The local event of the year. A heavenly gathering of all the charity angels of mercy.

"Why are you bringing that up now, John?"

Brenda called this morning when you were asleep. I told her I'd get back to her. What do you want me to tell her?

"Tell her to shove that fake smile up her bony ass..."

What?

"Tell her we'll be there," she says cordially. "It was nice of her to invite us. And tell her I'll call her in a couple of days. You told her I was sick, right?"

You are sick, he thinks, and ready for the nut house...

You're not comin' out of that room, are you?

Silence.

Since around Christmastime, almost a year ago, Vera had been retreating to her bedroom. To sleep. But she did come out every so often. To stroll the grounds of her country estate. Through the cold winter, the spring and summer, and into this present fall, she had come out when the mood struck her. To see a good-hearted young man she knew. To talk to him. And it had not gone unnoticed. Even as John Evans left his wife alone to return to his own affairs, he thought about it.

Lady Vera hardly ever goes into the world anymore.

Except to walk.

27

*T*here are those who skip through life on a rose petal carpet. Moving effortlessly across the years by privileges, and the advantages afforded by birth. Through no fault of their own, they go from one point of happiness to the next with the dim, sedated look of complacency in their eyes. The joy of life plastered over contented expressions. Every so often, the rose path knows a space of loneliness and heartache, and they bewail to the heavens about the little sorrow. A few hours, a few days of sadness is an eternity, even causing regret for times of origin. But they soon reach the next point of happiness, and quickly forget this brief sorrow and misery.

But for some, *birth* begins the Lonely Season—

And these quickly discover that their path is littered with thistles, while they move painfully from one point of suffering to the next. And they might travel across all the years to their graves, without ever realizing the most horrific portion of the truth…

That the greater part of their suffering was caused by *other people.*

Even here, in the bedroom of this isolated house, this curious fact goes unheralded. I cast no blame, as I gaze through the window that was nailed shut a year ago. I lasted through that cold, gray winter. Through the new, sadistic abuses and long periods of starvation.

I had studied the trees through the window frame, until I noticed leaf and flower buds appear. The days seem longer, the birds noisier and more plentiful. Rains came and watered the forests and fields, giving them strength and nourishment for their rebirth. I watch the trees develop their flowers, which soon fall into spring breezes. Through the window, shades of green contrast fluffy white clouds, and the deep blue skies of late spring and summer.

The warm summer wind blew colder, and the skies outside my window were gray again. The days grow shorter, the green woods begin to show their true colors. Then my western breeze returns from its journey around the Earth, plucking the dead autumn leaves and flinging them angrily to the ground. The trees are skeletons once again, having already gone to sleep for another winter.

Though I have watched the flow of seasons, and even felt the changing weather in my body, my soul has remained in my winter's prison, and I remember the knife, and the burning like it was yesterday.

This tenth year of my marriage has been one long winter. Every day of which was spent imprisoned in this room.

Wasting away. In the painful acceptance that perhaps…

There is only Fate.

ABOUT THE AUTHOR

Jonathan Lovejoy is a graduate of the University of North Carolina at Greensboro, with a B.A. in Religious Studies, and a graduate of Liberty University with an M.A. in Theological Studies. He currently lives in Winston Salem, North Carolina.

For more info on the author's life and career, visit jonathanlovejoy.com.

www.ingramcontent.com/pod-product-compliance
Lightning Source LLC
Chambersburg PA
CBHW060613130626
46555CB00002B/514